To The Cove
The Beginning

Tammy Bradley

Dedicated to my grands

Special thanks to Cynthia Bradley

Check out the whole series

The Dragon's Cove

The Wolf King

Back To The Cove; Barrett's Legacy

To The Cove; The Beginning

Mateo (In progress)

Copyrighted June 9, 2024

Tammy Bradley@

To The Cove

The Beginning

"Crimes of this severity are deemed worthy of death. He should be executed!" Yori slammed his first down on the table.

"Yori, he's our brother." Samuel rebutted.

"If it had been any other man an axe would have already taken his head." Yori argued folding his arms in front of his chest. "Your Majesty, tell me I am wrong?" Yori added turning to face his king.

"You are not but Jack is not of sound mind, Yori." King Idris reminded him. "And I find it a little disturbing that you desire your brother's execution." Idris said as he sat on his throne.

"I don't desire his death." Yori said gripping the chair in front of him tightly. He sighed before speaking, calming his tone. "But he will never stop. If we don't end this now another girl will die. I cannot live with that, Sam." Yori turned and looked at his brother. "Jack is the byproduct of our father's infidelity with a woman of wolf blood. He should have never been conceived but here we are before our king with a dilemma that shouldn't even be a discussion."

"I will not agree to his demise, Yori." Samuel stood facing his brother.

"If we don't do something he will do it again. Figure something out Samuel or I will have no choice but to take matters into my own hands." Yori said calmly warning him.

"Yori, are you making threats in front of our king? How will that look for you if something happens to Jack?" Samuel asked, pointing at Yori. Yori walked toward the door, turned and bowed to Idris, then left the room. Jack was sitting in a chair with shackles confining him. Two of the King's guards stood on either side of him, when Yori stepped into the hallway. Jack's head was tilted forward with his hair covering his face.

He had an evil smile when he spoke. "I guess your choice was not an option? I have not done enough bad that warrants my death?"

Yori put his hand lovingly on the top of Jack's head. "I am sorry Jack. I tried. I know that this won't end until you do. I see your pain, brother but they do not." Yori said with remorse. "I do love you, Jack." Yori smiled and patted his brother's back.

Jack leaned against him. "I know you do."

"Goodbye Jack." Yori said and walked away.

"I won't remember your kindness big brother." Jack shouted after him.

Yori looked over his shoulder and smiled. "I know Jack. I know."

******

"Samuel, can you present me with a reasonable resolution to our problem with Jack?" Idris asked after Yori left the room.

"If we did execute Jack, it would cause an uprising in the wolf kingdom, sire. I think our best option is to lock him up in the lower dungeons." Samuel said resting his hand on the hilt of his sword.

Idris tapped his chin in thought. "Yes, I will agree to that. Have them bring him forth." Samuel motioned the guards to bring Jack in. The chains clanked as Jack shuffled his feet. The guards staying at his side turned him to face the king.

"Jack because of my fondness for your family you will not be executed but instead spend the rest of your natural life in the belly of the dudgeon." Idris said as Jack stood up straight and tossed his hair back so he could see.

"If you are waiting for a thank you there won't be one. And Samuel, if you had any balls, you would have stood with Yori and had me beheaded. You think that imprisoning me will stop me? Something locked up is eventually freed whether it is intended or not." Jack whipped his head around to Samuel. "And that little Jenna, she's going to be mine someday." Jack said and licked his lips.

"Get him out of my sight." Idris said with disdain waving him away.

"Tootles big brother." Jack laughed as the guards drug him out the door.

"I hope this was the best decision because it sure doesn't feel like it is." Idris said standing.

******

"What happened with Jack?" Clara asked Yori when he entered their room.

He sat down at his desk. "Not the way we had hoped." He said picking up his pen. He opened the scroll in front of him and started writing. "I don't know what my father was thinking knowing that his human and her wolf blood would not bond." Clara walked over to him and rubbed his shoulders. "Where are the boys?" He asked, swinging her around and into his lap.

"Well, Ezra is practicing his blade skills, Grayson went riding with Joe, and Barrett walked down to the kitchen to steal a cookie." She said in between the kisses he gave her.

"So, we may have a moment or two?" He grinned winking at her. Quickly, he untied her bodice on her dress and freed her breasts from their bondage. "Hello ladies." Yori smiled burying his face between them.

******

"Hello Barrett." King Idris greeted the small boy who was carrying a handful of cookies. When Barrett bowed one of his cookies came loose from his grip. Idris caught the treat before it hit the floor.

"Good catch, your majesty!" Barrett shouted surprised.

"May I keep this one?" Idris asked as they continued walking.

"Sure!" Barrett answered shoving a cookie in his mouth.

"Thank you, the Queen won't let me have them you know." He said turning the cookie over looking at both sides.

"How come?" Barrett asked confused as to why she begrudged the king a cookie."

"She thinks I will get fat." Idris took a bite and rubbed his belly. "Very good."

"Ummhum." Barrett agreed.

Idris laughed at him. "You are a fun boy. I came to see your father; may I walk with you?" Barrett nodded his head. "Will you join the King's army when you are of age Barrett, like your brothers?"

"Yes, my Lord, I have been practicing." Barrett said then hung his head. "But not with a real sword though. Father said I'm not big enough yet."

"Well, he's right you know. Keep practicing and you will be

as good as he is." Idris said ruffling the boy's hair.

"Father!" Barrett shouted as he opened the door. "King Idris is here to see you." When Idris entered, he realized he had caught them in an intimate moment and turned his back. Clara jumped up from Yori's lap and stood behind him as she tucked herself away.

"I apologize for the intrusion." Idris said giving them a moment.

"My Lord, would you care to walk outside? I think I could use some fresh air." Yori suggested standing slowly.

"Yes, I do believe you do." Idris understood the condition he was in at the moment. "Oh, and Lady Clara," Idris said as he turned to leave. "Lilly asked for your family's company this evening for supper."

"Thank you, my Lord." Clara curtsied.

Yori closed the door behind them, and they headed down the hall. "Are you alright?" Idris asked with a chuckle as Yori adjusted himself.

"Yes, your Majesty." Yori answered shaking his head. "That woman can set me on fire quicker than anything."

"I didn't like the way you left today." Idris said looking up at the sky as they stepped outside.

"My apologies, I felt it was better to leave than to say more to offend you." Yori said sincerely.

"Yori, I do see your side of it and you were right when you said had it been any man but Jack he would have been executed. But causing a rip tide within the wolf community could cause war. The best case scenario for the time being is his imprisonment. Him being forgotten is what is best for everyone." Idris said as they walked over to where their sons battled against one another.

"Everyone but Jack. Even through his madness he realizes he should die." Yori gripped the hilt of his sword.

"Let's lay this discussion to rest, Yori. It will get us nowhere today." Idris calmly ordered. He stood for a moment his hands together in front of himself as he watched the sparing. "Ezra is very good Yori. I dare say almost as talented as you."

"That's saying a lot considering my brother's reputation." Samuel said as he joined the conversation.

"He is to join us on the next excursion." Idris told Yori. "He is ready." Yori nodded at him that he understood. "Marcus stand out." Idris shouted to his son. "I want to see what young Ezra does against a seasoned swordsman. Yori."

Idris motioned for Yori to exchange places with Marcus.

"Do not hold back on the boy Yori. See what he's got." Samuel winked.

"Father." Ezra smiled as Yori entered the ring.

"Ezra." Yori said exchanging greetings. Ezra swung his sword in circles at his side in anticipation of this battle with his father. Yori had been training his sons since they were small, but Ezra had a love for the sword and he was very talented.

"This should be interesting." Charles said, taking his gloves off and bowed when he approached the king. Charles had fought beside the king for many years as one of his most respected and honored soldiers.

"Indeed, it should." Idris agreed. Ezra began with the first strike against his father. Yori blocked the blow and returned an offensive strike with force. Ezra stood his ground and countered with two consecutive swings. The battle continued with Ezra showing his strength. Yori threw one strike after the other backing Ezra up until he fell. Yori stopped with his blade just stopping at his son's chest.

"Bravo! Bravo!" Idris cheered. Ezra pushed the sword a side embarrassed of his fall. Yori held out his hand and helped Ezra up to his feet. Ezra stood prepared for another round.

"Are you sure, son?" Yori asked Ezra.

"Watch this." Marcus told Samuel smacking his arm. Ezra tilted his head to the side and smiled. He backed Yori up with a couple of well placed blows and his father returned the favor. The next move was a jab forward, the one Ezra was waiting for. One handed Ezra maneuvered his wrist to circle Yori's blade causing his father to lose control and drop his sword. Ezra stepped forward and placed the tip of his blade at the base of his father's throat.

"Yield?" Ezra grinned with pride.
"Yield." Yori answered and clapped his hands. Whistles and laughter were heard around the arena. Yori bowed to his son. "I am impressed. That is a well played maneuver. You must teach me sometime."

"And so the teacher becomes the student." Charles said when Ezra and Yori walked up to the group.

Marcus slipped away to the stables and saddled his horse. "I will be back soon father." Marcus said as he rode up to Idris.

"Marcus don't keep your mother waiting for supper." Idris shook a finger at him. "She will squabble at me for months if you're late."

"I will be there." He grinned and urged his horse onward. It was a pleasant ride to the river. A nice breeze blew against the horse's mane, cooling him in the summer heat. Marcus was excited. He hadn't seen her in almost a week. A smile crossed his face as he pictured her dark complected skin and long auburn hair. Her green eyes seemed to change the rhythm of his heart every time he looked at her. The young prince whistled a tune as he rode down the path. Marcus noticed the newly oncoming nervousness of his animal that let him know she was already there. Stopping the horse, he tied it to a sapling and walked the rest of the way on foot. He saw her sitting by the edge of the river with her feet dangling in the water. Silently, he eased his steps, moving with careful intent, trying to sneak up on her.

"Marcus, I know you're there." She said turning her head with a beautiful smile.

"Ahh, Angelina you heard my heart leaping from my chest again. I will never be able to catch you unaware." Marcus said sliding up next to her stealing a kiss.

"It is not your heart, my love but those loud strides of yours." She laughed. "I have missed you." She took the crown from his head and placed it on hers. He chuckled when it fell forward and settled on the bridge of her nose.

"I don't think it fits." She shrugged.

"No, but a crown made for a princess would." He smiled but she did not return the gesture. Her frown disheartened him.

"You know we can never marry, Marcus." She said interlacing her fingers in his. "Our families will never allow it to be. I can just see the king's face when you tell him you are bringing a wolf into his court."

"So, I'll renounce my crown. Simple." Marcus shrugged and kissed the top of her hand.

"Simple is never an adjective I would use with your family Marcus. Besides, our blood would never bond so we could never have children." She said laying her hand softly on the side of his face.

"Are you ending our relationship?" He asked with fear.

"No, not at all. I just don't know how to make it work yet." She smiled as she looked into his brown eyes. Gathering her skirts she straddled his lap. "I love you, Marcus, with all my heart. I want to be with you forever." She kissed his forehead and rolled her hips around on him. "It has been too long without you, lover." He moaned when she gently pulled at his lip with her teeth.

"Are we good not to make a babe?" Marcus asked feeling her unbuttoning his pants under her skirt. "I guess we are." Marcus grinned when she freed him. His hands reached for her bottom and pulled her closer. She rushed her lips into his hard and her fangs broke the skin on his lip. He smiled through the passionate kisses. He loved her wild forceful wanting. Her head flew back when he pulled her onto him. She cried out and looked at him with those wicked green eyes as she lowered her top. He cupped her very blessed breasts in his hands and nuzzled them. Her nails raked his back as he laid her down on the grass and slowed their passion down to a gentle love. After a few moments of cuddling, he stood and helped her to stand. Walking down to the river they jumped in to cool their bodies.

"I love you." Marcus whispered in her ear as he kissed her neck.

"More of that and you will be spending the night." She said wrapping her arms around his waist.

" I only wish that I could but I'm going to have to head back my queen. I cannot be late today." Marcus said already regretting his departure.

"You are a grown man. Why must you still answer to your father?" She asked with a pout.

"Because, my love, my father is the King. My mother has invited influential families to the table tonight. My presence was demanded." He answered holding her close nibbling her neck.

She touched his lip where she drew blood feeling the swollen bump from the trauma. She gently kissed it. "I am sorry I hurt you."

"It doesn't hurt." He lied. "Angelina, I don't want to live without you. Let me talk to my father about a marriage."

"It is not just your family that we need to convince, Marcus. Do I need to remind you of the plight that Jack's creation caused? Here we sit in a possible similar situation." She lifted his head when he lowered it. "Make no mistake about it I am madly in love with you and would give up babies to be your wife, but this is not going to be easy."

"Nothing worthwhile is. WE will find a way I promise." He said and led her out of the water. "I must be going Angelina. Send word when we can meet again." He said as they dressed.

"I will my love." She kissed him and set his crown upon his head. He kissed her one more time and smacked her bottom. As she turned to leave, she morphed into her wolf and trotted into the woods. He watched until she was out of sight before heading back to his horse and began to sing a song kicking up his heels once as he walked down the path. He noticed his horse's attention shift in a different direction and slowed his pace becoming more attentive to his surroundings. The horse was getting nervous which led him to believe there were wolves close by. He spoke to the animal trying to ease its fears.

"Prince Marcus." A familiar voice called out to him. When he turned Angelina's brother was there and two others who he believed were her cousins.

"Austin." Marcus acknowledged him keeping his demeanor social.

"I thought we had an understanding concerning my sister." He said with his hands on his hips.

"We do. I understand that you don't approve and you understand that I couldn't give two rat's tail ends whether you do or not." Marcus laughed and clapped his hands. "Look Austin, Angelina and I know what we're doing."

"No, man I don't think you do." Austin motioned his cousins over to Marcus's sides.

"Austin, you don't want to do this." Marcus said shaking his head and chuckling.

"Ya I believe I do. You see your royal blood means nothing to the pack and you are on wolf soil." Austin said angry with Marcus's cocky attitude.

"So far all I hear is talk." Marcus bantered. "Step up!" Austin lunged at Marcus with a right hook to his eye and an uppercut to the jaw. The cousins held Marcus firmly. A jab to the ribs took his breath away. "Ok, that one kind of hurt." Marcus said bending over laughing. He looked around when he heard riders behind him.

"Prince Marcus, I do believe you are having fun without us." Joe said still sitting on his horse. "Isn't he Grayson?"

"He is indeed." Grayson said dismounting his horse.

"There's plenty to go around." Marcus said and spat blood. Joe jumped off his horse and pulled his gloves tighter on his hands.

"Let's make it a fair game." Grayson said as he and Joe sucker punched the cousins simultaneously. They released Marcus and he took the opportunity and speared Austin in the gut with his shoulder. The cousins regained their senses and threw punches at Grayson and Joe. Austin transformed and called the cousins. They morphed and stood by Austin growling and bearing their fangs. "Alright! That's enough!" Grayson shouted pulling his sword. "We've all had a bit of fun. But you are threatening a Prince of the royal court. This ends now!" Grayson walked in front of Marcus and stood with his blade, ready for battle. Joe tossed Marcus up on his horse while Grayson watched their backs. Joe mounted his horse and grabbed Marcus's reins. He whistled at Grayson. Grayson backed up to his horse and mounted it his sword still drawn. His horse was pawing at the ground nervous to leave. Grayson shouted and jump started his horse.

******

"Your son is late." The Queen advised King Idris with a frown.

"My dear, how is it that he is always my son when his behavior is lacking manners?" Idris asked leaning back in his chair. "I am sure he will be here soon."

"The King's son isn't the only one lacking in manners." Clara quietly spoke looking at Yori and Samuel. Marcus ran his fingers through his hair as he walked into the dining hall with Joe and Grayson. They quickly took their seats not making eye contact with anyone.

"We will enjoy this wonderful meal before we discuss your tardiness and your appearance." Idris said with an easy tone. Ezra looked at Grayson and grinned over the black eye on his face and the look on their mother's face. She was not pleased at all.

"Mother, Grayson has a black eye." Barrett tattled.

"So, he does." She said stirring her food around in her plate.

"Tattletale." Grayson whispered to his little brother and stole a biscuit from Barrett's plate. Barrett stuck his tongue out at Grayson then quickly looked at his mother to see if she had caught him.

Idris watched Lilly push her plate away from in front of her. "You must try to eat, my dear." Idris said pushing it back to her.

"My Lord, this babe of yours does flip flops turning my stomach sour. I cannot eat at the moment." She said quietly. Clara could tell he was worried for her wellbeing. She had lost too much weight.

"I think we should take a ride to the northern border soon." Idris said opening a different topic of conversation. "It has been a while since anyone has been there. It would give young Ezra here a chance to see what it's like to ride with us."

"It has been a while indeed, your Majesty." Samuel

agreed.

"If I remember correctly, it had some great fields that were full of wheat." Charles said looking down the table at the king.

"Yes, it would be a great place to farm and establish a community." Idris answered.

"Your Majesty, if I may?" Ezra spoke up and when Idris acknowledged him, he continued. "Hasn't there been raids along that road?"

"Yes, Ezra there has but no more than any other outside path that leads away from the safety of the kingdom. Thinking like a soldier already." Idris looked at Yori. "I like it." The chatter continued until their meal was finished, the Queen rose everyone followed suit, standing respectfully,

"Good evening gentlemen. Ladies if you would like to join me in the sewing room we shall have some tea." Lilly said folding her hands together and waited for Clara and Marcy to join her.

"Come along Barrett." Clara said holding out her hand to him.

"I don't want to have tea mother." Barrett pouted crossing

his arms in front of him.

"It is fine, Lady Clara to let the boy stay." Idris said dismissing them and winking at Barrett. "That's ok young sir I would not want to have tea either."

"Father, I would have been back on time had I not been jumped on the way back." Marcus said beginning the dreaded conversation. "And Joe and Grayson stopped to help me."

"You were in the wolf territory again, wasn't you?" Idris asked shaking his head. "I have asked you time and time again to break it off with her. How can you have sons to be king if you marry a wolf?" You should start thinking less like a horney teenager and more like a future king." Idris said addressing his son.

"What if I had rather marry Angelina than be king? If Lincoln had lived it would be his to inherit. I never wanted it. Give it to Henry!" Marcus said raising his voice.

"Marcus." Yori said addressing his attitude toward his father.

"My apologies Father." Marcus nodded to his father. "I did not mean to bring Lincoln into it. My brother was a good man."

"Lincoln's death was honorable and I miss him dearly but Henry although very intelligent does not have the strength that a king needs in battle." Idris rebuked.

"Then Ezra, he has the presence of a king. Let him take the crown after you." Marcus said gesturing to Ezra.

"I don't understand why it is so forbidden. Why must we have segregation with the wolf people." Joe asked. "How fair is it not to spend your life with the one you love?"

"Joe, you too?" Samuel snapped his head around to his son when he realized he was talking about himself as well. "I forbid it. Do you not think this family has been through enough with Jack? He is the beginning and the end of any reasons why humans and wolves should not pair!" Samuel reiterated tossing down his fork. Yori looked at Grayson, who was still eating. He felt eyes upon him and looked around the table. He laid his silverware down politely and wiped his mouth with a napkin. Ezra rolled his eyes at Grayson's theatrics.

"I was just there for support. I don't nor do I wish to have a girlfriend from the wolf nation." Grayson said matter of factly.

"That's because he doesn't have a girlfriend." Barrett giggled.

"Barrett." Yori scolded. "If you to stay, keep quiet."

"Yes, Father." Barrett answered snatching his biscuit back from Grayson's plate.

"What of you Ezra?" Yori asked, turning toward his oldest.

"I do have a girlfriend, but she is not wolf. She lives in the village of Elder Andrew. In fact, she is his eldest daughter, Asia." Ezra said proudly.

"Always having to be the star child huh Ezra?" Joe spat. "Future king right there." He waved in Ezra's direction.

"That is not fair Joe." Grayson said standing. "Ezra and I both have been there for you and Marcus at different times."

"Tis true." Marcus agreed. "Father please think upon this matter. That's all I am asking." Marcus said looking at Idris with his hand covering his heart. Idris nodded in agreement and dismissed the young men from the table.

******

"Would you like me to pour you some tea my Lady?" Lilly's

handmaiden asked.

"No, I don't want any tea, thank you." She gathered her skirts, slipped off her shoes and curled up on the couch. Come on ladies you don't really think I called you in here to sew or drink tea did you? I want juicy details of your love and sex lives." Lilly laughed rubbing her tiny hands together. Marcy and Clara smiled and sat down on pillows in the floor.

"Well, your grace, your husband, caught Yori nose deep in my breasts earlier today." Clara confessed with an embarrassed giggle.

"No!" Lilly said covering her mouth.

"Yes, I was all outside my bodice. I am sure he saw them all perky and excited. But being the gentleman the king is he immediately turned his back.

"That is my Idris. But ladies he is a wild man in the bedroom I assure you." Lilly said, fanning her face.

"Charles is the more subtle romantic type. I am the one who is a little risqué." Marcy said raising her eyebrows up and down.

"Marcy!" Clara giggled.

"Girls! You've got to try it sometime. Take control one night, surprise him. Trust me he will love it." Marcy said winking.

"Oh, that reminds me." Lilly said as she turned toward her lady. "I have something for you." Her lady handed each of her friends a bottle of perfume. "This is from across the sea. It has a special mixture that seems to drive the men wild with desire."

"It smells wonderful." Clara said after smelling the sweet aroma.

"Like you need any help, Clara. After three boys your body still looks great." Marcy said as she smelled her opened bottle.

******

"Ezra, man I am sorry about that." Joe said shaking his cousin's hand.

"No hard feelings Joe." Ezra said sincerely.

"Well, I'm going to take off. Thanks again for today." Marcus waved as he headed off down the hall.

"I am going to hide out somewhere for a while till father cools down. He didn't know about Julie until now. I'm sure he has plenty more to say." Joe tilted his head to the side smiling. "See you tomorrow cousins." He added pointing both his index fingers at them as he left their group.

"Grayson, I am heading out to see Asia. Would you join me?" Ezra asked with a smile that stretched across his face.

"I am not covering for another one of you boys so you can get your jollys." Grayson said taking Barrett's hand.

"Grayson what is jollys? Can I have some?" Barrett asked looking up at his brother.

"When you're older bub." Grayson said and starting walking away from Ezra.

"Gray, she's bringing a friend." Ezra said grinning as Grayson stopped and turned around.

"She had better be pretty." Grayson warned.

******

"They are but boys, your Majesty. I'm sure this will pass." Yori said dismissively.

"Easy for you to say brother your sons do not dabble in love with wolves." Samuel pouted.

"And by the look of the bruises on them I would venture to say the wolves are not amused as well." Idris said remaining seated. "Marcus is convinced that he is in love with Angelina. I must consider his chosen match. It possibly could create a union between our kingdoms."

"Without producing a son." Samuel added reminding him.

"Marcus is the only heir that would be the king our country needs. If my wife gives me another son, he then will be king after Marcus. This is reasonable." Idris stood. Samuel was not pleased. He understood the pain Jack had caused his family and it angered him that his son chose a wolf to love. He had to stop this relationship.

"When would you like to ride to the northern border, my Lord?" Samuel asked.

"Let's plan in four days. I will be free of any obligations, and we can take our time. Now if you will excuse me, I have plans with Lilly for the evening." Idris nodded at them and left the room.

******

"Ezra if Asia is alone, I will not wait on you." Grayson warned as they rode to her village.

"Don't worry she sent word that is why I asked you to come." Ezra winked at his brother. "Look, there in the water. Her name is Vada and she is staying with Asia's family now. I'm not sure of the reasons but it doesn't matter." He nodded in the direction of the girls. "They bathe nude." Ezra and Grayson dismounted and tied down their horses. Ezra kneeled on one knee and pulled a piece of dead grass from the ground. They watched the girls bathing until Asia caught them.

"Ezra, son of Yori are you spying on us." Asia asked smiling.

"Yes, my Lady. I have been caught red handed." Ezra had been sweet on Asia for a long time and knew from the moment he saw her she would be his.

"Hello Grayson, this is Vada." Asia introduced. Grayson had been leaning up against a tree and stood upright when Vada turned around. A smile slowly spread over his face when he saw her big black eyes and long braided hair.

"My Lady." Grayson slightly bowed. His smile forced his

dimples to emerge. Vada looked down blushing at the way he looked at her.

"Are you staying on dry ground starring or will you join me in the water Ezra?" Asia asked splashing at him.

"Maybe, I am pretty content with watching you bathe." He said as he tugged on his braided beard.

"That's too bad then because we were just finishing up." She said looking up at him with a wicked smile.

"In that case I could join you for a few moments." Ezra pulled off his shirt as he stood and laid his sword down. He started to undo his pants then looked at Vada. "I am not shy Vada to warn you." Ezra said as his pants dropped to the ground. Vada spun around and covered her eyes. After hearing a splash behind her, Vada turned back around to see what Grayson was doing.

"My Lady, I know we have just met so if you had rather I will stay where I am." Grayson kneeled to one knee.

"You are very kind sir, but it would be easier to have a conversation with you if you were closer." Vada said raising up a little out of the water just enough that he could see the top of her breasts.

"Very well." Grayson pulled his shirt over his head and she

smiled at his well developed shoulders. She turned her head slightly when he removed his pants but not enough she couldn't see his whole body. Ezra and Asia had moved to a more secluded spot giving both couples some privacy.

"I have missed you." Ezra smiled kissing her lips. Asia put her arm around his neck and pressed her body against him.

"I can tell." She said amused feeling him swollen against her.

"Asia," Ezra said twirling a strand of her hair around his finger. He looked to the sky and grinned before lowering his eyes to hers. "I love you." He finally conveyed.

She caressed the side of his face. "I love you too, Ezra." She confessed. Ezra pressed his lips against hers as he lifted her up onto him. She locked her legs around his waist as they sank into deeper water.

"Well, they make no secret about their intensions do they?" Vada asked turning her back to them.

"No, they do not leave anything to the imagination. If it bothers you, we can go for a walk." Grayson offered standing in front of her but not touching.

"I am fine." She moved closer and ran her fingers over his

massive biceps and his shoulders. "You are also with the king's army?"

"I am." Grayson smiled as she traced his lips with her fingertip.

"Are you going to kiss me?" Vada asked letting her finger slide down his chin. She looked up at him through her black eyes and he lifted his face to the sky.

"Have mercy!" Grayson said as he lowered his lips to hers. Vada took his hand and brought it up to her breast. Her hand wondered down his chest and past his waist. "Vada, are you sure?" Grayson asked when he felt her touch him.

"You are my first, but you are the one I chose." Vada said kissing him.

"Come with me." Grayson took her to a secluded grassy knoll and laid her down softly. He brushed her cheek tenderly and looked into her eyes. She pulled his face down to meet hers hungry for them to be together.

"Grayson, please." She begged as she reached for him, but he stopped her.

"Not yet." He said as he placed kisses down her neck and to each breast. Her hips rose up to him inviting, urging. His kisses didn't stop at her belly and she cried out when he reached her sweet spot.

"Well, it sounds like they are having fun." Ezra chuckled when hearing Vada.

"So it seems. I was hoping they would hit it off." Asia giggled.

"It may be a few days until I can see you again." Ezra said kissing her neck lovingly. "The king plans a trip to the northern border soon and has said that I am to go." Ezra said softly playing with her breasts.

"That road is dangerous, Ezra. Rumors of raids are always being reported." She said concerned then gasped when he found her below the waterline.

"I will be safe, Asia. I ride with the greatest of swordsmen. No one would dare cross blades with any of them." He helped her up on the bank and followed her up. Laying beside her Ezra snuggled up to her. "I can't believe how beautiful you are?" He said as he kissed her gently. Asia raised her leg over his hips pulling him in even closer to her. "You're going to start something again that I don't have time for. I have training this evening so I must go." He said regretfully and kissed her nose.

When he stood, she giggled. "Are you sure you shouldn't take care of that before you leave." He looked down at the issue she was referring to.

"That happens a lot when I'm around you." Ezra smiled at her picking up his pants.

"I could take care of that for you." She said and kneeled before him.

******

"What is wrong Barrett?" Clara asked her pouting son. She sat beside him on the couch and brushed his hair back from his face.

"Ezra and Grayson went to see Asia and they left me here." He said and sat in his mother's lap. "It's not fair I never get to do anything."

"Why don't you find your father and we shall go to the marketplace. Maybe find some sweets?" Clara said hugging him.

"Really?" Barrett asked climbing down from her lap, he headed to the door. "I'll be back with Father." Barrett smiled at his mother and tried to wink at her. She winked back then stood to fix her hair in the mirror. She remembered the perfume the Queen had given her earlier and took it from her pocket. She bit her lip thinking about the reaction she might receive from Yori. Taking off the cork she dabbed a faint amount on her wrists and behind her ears.

"Barrett said you requested my presence to go to the market for sweets." Yori said as he walked passed her to his desk. He stopped mid stride when he caught the smell of her perfume. He looked at her from the corner of his eyes. She acted as though she hadn't noticed his attention to the fragrance and fussed with her hair. Yori walked up behind her wrapping his arms around her waist. He smelled the back of her ear.

"What's this that makes my loins ache?" Yori asked kissing the back of her neck.

"It's just a little rose water husband that is all." She said shrugging her shoulders.

"Maybe, it's just your beauty that encourages me to bed you." Yori turned her around to face him kissing her passionately. Clara felt a tug at her skirt. She looked down at Barrett who was standing there his arms crossed and he was mad.

"Barrett, are you ready to go?" She asked him.

"Woman you have left me in a position that I shouldn't leave the room in once again." Yori rolled his head and rubbed his neck. She smiled wickedly at him and opened the door.

"Come along Barrett." Clara said taking his hand. She could hear Yori muttering unhappily as he closed the door behind them. They met Idris and Lilly in the hallway inviting their company.

Clara put her arm around the Queens waist and whispered to her as they walked. "My Lady, the perfume works."

"You're wearing it?" Lilly whispered back. "Harlet, teasing your man so." She laughed.

******

"Why did you come back, Marcus?" Austin asked angrily as he slammed his fist into the prince's midsection. Marcus raised his finger up to pause the conversation as he bent over and puked.

After wiping off his mouth he stood slowly. "I came to get your sister, Austin. She will be my queen on day. Just think about it. This union could benefit both of our kingdoms for years to come." Austin nodded and two of his men tied Marcus to a tree. "Come on man. Do we really need to do this again?"

"You were told to stay away. If my father finds out you were here prince or not you would be torn apart." Austin said as he threw another punch. Blood flew from Marcus's lip as Austin's fist landed on his mouth. Marcus spat and touched the cut with his tongue.

"That was a good one." Marcus chuckled. Austin broke ribs with the next jab he wielded Marcus.

"Agree you will never see my sister again." Austin said pulling on his hair raising his head up to see his face.

"How fair is it to ask to give up the one who gives purpose to your life? I stand here and take your beatings hoping you will see that I would do anything for her." Marcus said through labored breaths. The next hit Marcus took was at his eyebrow splitting it open. All Marcus did was laugh. He could do no more than that. Austin took an arrow from his quiver.

"Come on Marcus, give." Austin said rubbing his face. Marcus blinked the blood away that ran into his eye. There was wheezing in his laugh when he looked at Angelina's brother. Austin placed the arrowhead against Marcus's chest and pressed in.
"Do it!" Marcus dared leaning his chest into the arrow. "Because that's what it's going to take to make me stop coming for her." Austin walked away from him picking up his bow. He looked at Marcus for a moment and pulled

back the string.

"No! Austin, please no!" Angelina screamed running in front of Marcus. "Brother, I love him." Angelina begged.

"I know. Move her." He ordered his men.

"Angelina, I love you." Marcus said looking through bloody swollen eyes. She looked from Marcus to her brother and when she saw the arrow leave the bow she slipped away from her captors and in front Marcus. The arrow went into her back and through her heart into Marcus's heart pinning them together.

She looked into his eyes. Now we can be together forever." She laid her head upon his shoulder as she died.

Marcus smiled as he looked at Austin. "Told you I wasn't leaving without her." Smiling Marcus looked back at Angelina kissed her cheek then followed her into the stars. Austin lowered his head and screamed. He had taken his sister's life and the life of a crowned prince. He had just started a war.

******

Yori held Clara's hand as they walked through the

marketplace with King Idris and Queen Lilly. Barrett walked along beside them eating chocolate that was given to him by a vendor.

"Your Majesties." A couple bowed as they approached.

"Lady Sara!" Lilly said, tickled to see her. Her husband Andrew joined Yori and the king talking while the women caught up. Barrett walked over to Sara's little girl to say hi.

"Want some chocolate?" Barrett asked her holding out the melting treat.

"Sure." She answered, taking a piece he broke off for her.

"What's your name?" Barrett asked her.

"Jenna, what is yours?" She asked biting a on the corner.

"Barrett, it's good right?" Barrett asked licking his lips.

"Mmmmhmmm." She agreed, shoving the block of chocolate into her mouth.

Sara looked at the children. "I'm assuming our other children are together somewhere."

"Barrett said Ezra and Grayson left to see Asia. I'm wondering if we won't become in laws soon. Clara said taking Sara's hand excited.

"A wedding would be a welcomed celebration." Lilly said fanning herself. Her face was bright red from the heat.

"Is Vada still staying with you?" Clara asked her friend.

"Yes Clara, why do you ask?" Sara asked huddling closer to Clara and Lilly.

"I was wondering why Grayson would ride with Ezra to see Asia unless it's because they wanted him to meet Vada." Clara said tapping her chin.

"She is still bound, isn't she?" Lilly asked in a gasp.

"Yes, she still wears the ambulant." Sara said and saw relief on Clara's face.

"As beautiful as Vada is my son will be smitten by her." Clara shook her head.

"What are you ladies gossiping about?" King Idris asked as they approached the women.

"We were thinking that the Queen was getting too warm." Clara winked at Lilly.

"She does look heated." Idris said and kissed her

forehead. "I'd say we've had enough fun tonight. What do you think my love?"

"I am ready." She agreed and they walked back to the castle.

Yori put his arms around his wife. "I'm thinking our fun is just beginning." He whispered to her.

"Barrett say bye to Jenna." Clara said taking Barrett's hand. He waved to her with the hand still holding his chocolate. "Sara we'll talk soon." She smiled at her friend.

"What was that all about?" Yori asked placing his hand at the small of her back.

"Apparently, Ezra took Grayson to meet Vada this evening." Clara informed him.

"No." He chuckled. "That's a little ironic. Grayson confessed after supper he had no intentions of being with a woman from the wolf nation."

"I do not find the humor here Yori." She said looking cross at him.

"She is still bound. She doesn't even know she is wolf. Let them have their fun for now." Yori smiled at her and winked.

"Yori, you know Grayson's heart. It will break when he finds out." Clara frowned.

******

"She's going to be angry with you when she learns we've taken their clothes." Grayson told Ezra as they mounted their horses.

"Yeah but it will be a few days before I see her again. It'll give her something to fuss about." He chuckled grinning.

"You love her don't you Ezra?" Grayson asked as they trotted back home.

"I do Grayson. I think I'm going to ask her to marry me." Ezra said and glanced at Grayson's for his reaction.

"Congratulations, big brother!" Grayson said sincerely.

"How did things go with Vada? Did you bed her?" Ezra asked crossing his arms over the saddle horn, looking over at Grayson.

"No, I did not." He answered without a smile.

"You didn't think she was pretty? What? Come on Gray

spill it." Ezra said acting disappointed in Grayson's lack of divulging information.

"She's beautiful, Ezra. I just wanted to wait. It would have been her first time and it needs to be done right not on a river nest." Grayson shrugged.
"I get that, but I'm surprised she sure was enjoying something." Ezra shook his head.

"Yes, my dear brother, she was." Grayson smiled and looked to the sky. "Have mercy!" He shouted and they sped up the horses to run.

******

Samuel woke Ezra and Grayson early the next morning.

"Ezra, King Idris would like to see you in the map room immediately. Grayson meet me in the stables. I have something for you and Joe to do for me." Samuel kicked Grayson's bunk. "Come on let's go." He said with irritation. He slammed the door on his way out without another word.

"He's cranky this morning." Ezra said slipping on his boots.

"He's always like that to me. For some reason he just doesn't like me." Grayson shrugged as he stood from his bed.

"Be careful today, Brother." Ezra said buckling his sword.

"As you, Ezra." Grayson said when Ezra left their room. Ezra knocked on the door of the map room and was told to enter.

"Good morning, your Majesty." Ezra said with a bow.

"Have you heard from Marcus?" The king asked as he spread out a map of the northern region on his desk.

"No, my Lord, not since supper yesterday." Ezra answered.

"Hmmm, well, I need you to hunt him down. It seems that no one has seen him." Idris looked up at Ezra. "You are his best friend; you know all his haunts. Please find my son."

"I will, my Lord." Ezra turned to leave and Idris spoke again.

"Don't tell him but I've decided to allow his marriage to Angelina." Idris smiled proudly.

"He will be very happy to hear that, your Majesty." Ezra

said with a nod.

"Ezra I can see potential in you. You will be my son's advisor someday." Idris said and put his nose back into the map.

"It would be an honor." Ezra smiled then left the room.

******

"The king is persistent about riding to the northern region. I want you two to ride it today. Don't engage in anything unless your life depends on it of course. I want to know of any raiders or wolves stalking that road." Samuel said as the boys mounted their horses.

"Father really? Wolves? They have their own territory what would they gain?" Joe asked pulling his hair back with a tie and started his horse forward.

Always needing to poke the bear huh Uncle?" Grayson asked Samuel taking the sack of food he handed to him.

"Be back by supper." Samuel said smacking the butt of his horse. A man strolled up to Samuel after Grayson rode off and took money from him.

"Make sure it looks like the wolves had something to do with it. Give them a good fight but don't kill them."

Samuel said sternly.

******

Ezra rode slow down the path towards the wolves' kingdom. Marcus had stirred up a stink by his constant pursuit of Angelina and Ezra was sure this is where he would find Marcus probably beaten up again or cuddled up with her. Ezra saw the ears of his horse perk up and he petted the animal's neck.

"Easy." Ezra tried to comfort him. A shadow followed him in the wood line. He was being watched. Ezra easily slipped his sword from its sheath and kept a wary eye to the side of him

"You have no business here, Ezra." The shadow finally spoke.

"I am on a mission for King Idris to find Prince Marcus." Ezra said slowly dismounting his horse. "Have you seen him?" Ezra asked as Austin walked into the light of the path and let the horse smell of his hand before answering.

"Yes, I know where he is." There was sadness in his voice or remorse that Ezra didn't understand yet. "Just over the hill." When they topped the hill Ezra saw them just as they were still joined by the arrow and Marcus bound to the tree. Ezra took in the scene and sighed there wasn't any need in Austin explaining. They continued forward not speaking, both burdened with sorrow. Ezra's friend had a frozen smile on his busted lips that lay gently on Angelina's cheek. A poetic love affair ending in tragedy becoming a kind of fulfillment that their love will indeed last forever. The image forever now burned into Ezra's mind saddened him but also gave him peace that his friend was now happy.

"You take yours and I'll take mine." Ezra said and helped him lay Angelina's body gently on the ground. Austin held Marcus up while Ezra cut his bonds, then laid him down by his Angelina. Ezra went to his saddle and retrieved a couple of blankets handing one to Austin.

"Ezra, I have arranged for you to take Marcus and leave unharmed. But my father will not tolerate another human in our kingdom." Austin said as he covered his sister.

"Your actions will cause conflict, Austin." Ezra said as they laid Marcus's body across Ezra's saddle.

"I know." Austin said as he walked away. Ezra took the reins of his horse and returned to the path. He thought about his friend, dead on the saddle behind him and clenched his jaw.

******

"I carved her name into my sword hilt, look Grayson." Joe said grinning as he pointed at it.

"You are ate up, Joe." Grayson said shaking his head.

"I am!" He laughed. "I love her." Joe shouted. Grayson turned to look behind them. "What is it?" Joe asked looking but seeing nothing.

"I don't know, something, maybe nothing." Grayson turned back around but pulled his sword and laid it across his lap.

"How did it go with Vada?" Joe asked, raising his eyebrows and winking.

"It was good." Grayson said and turned his head quickly to the side scanning the tree line. He noticed his horse's ear twitch in the same direction.

"Oh Cuz, you've got to give me more than that. What is it? Was she ugly?" Joe asked, watching a smile creep across Grayson's face.

"No, she's beautiful." Grayson covered his heart with his

hand and smiled remembering their moment.

"Did you bed her?" Joe asked, catching a piece of chicken Grayson tossed to him.

"Why is that always the question? Not that it is any of your business but no I did not." Grayson answered looking behind them again. "But that's not to say we didn't have any fun."

"Why are you so spooked?" Joe asked as Grayson turned back around in the saddle.

"I think we are being followed." Grayson said gripping the hilt of his sword.

"Wolves or human?" Joe asked pulling his own sword.

"Not sure yet." Grayson said as he picked up the pace of his horse. "Uncle Samuel was pretty angery when you told him of Julie. How are you going to work it out with him?" Grayson asked.

"It doesn't matter Gray. I am in love with her. If he can't accept it then we will just leave." Joe shrugged.

"Joe, Uncle Jack is pretty messed up in the head because of grandfather's bonding with a wolf. You'll never be able to have kids." Grayson warned.

"Yes, yes I know the story Grayson." Joe said irritated. "There must be a way."

"I hope so." Grayson stopped his horse. "I don't like the feel of this." Grayson watched his horse; he was nervous and stomped his foot anxious to move. Grayson felt a sharp stab in his back. He looked down to see an arrowhead protruding through his chest with blood dripping from the tip of it.

Joe looked over at him. "Well, that can't be good." He watched as three more arrows hit Grayson, the tips exiting his stomach. Joe reached for Grayson just as he felt the pain of arrows entering his back and neck and legs. Their frightened horses bucked and took off leaving their riders behind on the trail. Grayson tried to raise up to find Joe. He looked down at his stomach when he felt pain shoot through his body. The one through his chest caused him to gasp for air. He spat blood when he called out for his cousin.

"Joe!" One of Grayson's arms broke when he fell from the horse. Using the other arm he pulled himself over to Joe. Grayson coughed and blood poured from his mouth. "Joe." Grayson forced his voice. He looked at Joe's injuries. He saw the arrow sticking from Joe's neck and four had penetrated his chest. He had two arrows in each thigh as well that were bleeding badly.

"Grayson," Joe wheezed. "I'm dying. I can feel the blood pooling in my chest. I can't breathe. I don't want to drown." Joe gurgled the blood as he tried to talk. He turned his head, felt the arrow in his throat, and laughed. "Cousin please take my blade and finish me. Please." Joe's voice was but a whisper now and blood flowed from his mouth like a stream.

"I can't do that, Joe." Grayson begged feeling darkness taking over his conscious.

"Please don't let me drown." Joe pleaded placing a bloody hand on Grayson's arm. Grayson looked around finding Joe's sword at his side. "It's...ok." Joe said coughing up blood unable now to breath. Grayson saw the panic in Joe's eyes as the blood ran now from his nose. Grayson yelled as he plunged the sword into his cousin's chest. There was gratefulness in Joe's eyes as the light left them. Grayson cried out as he fell backwards. He looked at the sky taking his breaths in gasps feeling death's ugly hand reaching for him. His lasts thoughts were of Vada as his eyes closed.

******

When Ezra walked his horse to the edge of the

marketplace, he called to a young boy who was chopping wood nearby. Ezra handed him coin and asked him to find Lords Yori and Samuel and have them meet him in the stables. "Tell them Ezra asks for urgent assistance." Ezra added and walked to the wood line following it to avoid anyone curious of the load on his saddle. His father and Samuel were waiting for him when he arrived. Yori looked from his son to his saddle. His head dropped and he scratched his chin. Samuel walked over and threw back the blanket. Samuel covered Marcus and pinched the bridge of his nose.

"Where did you find him?" Samuel asked but already knew the answer.

"In the wolf community. He had been beaten. This time worse than before. Angelina was pinned to him an arrow through both of their hearts. It was Austin who killed them." Ezra explained. He tried to keep his composure. It wasn't easy. Those were his friend who were murdered after all.

Charles came in behind them bringing two riderless horses. "Yori, Samuel these horses came running through the marketplace without riders."

"That's my brother's horse." Ezra said walking up to the animal and rubbed his neck. "Father there is a lot of blood on Grayson's saddle." Samuel looked over Joe's horse and found blood on the saddle and down the side of the horse.

What had he done? Fear enveloped his nerves and he felt sick. Yori saw Samuel's face turn white.

"Where did you send the boys, Samuel?" Yori asked his brother. When he did not answer Yori shouted. "Samuel! Where did you send Joe and Grayson?"

"I sent them down the northern pass." Samuel answered. Yori found his horse and began to saddle it.

"I want to go Father." Ezra said earnestly.

"Ezra, I need you to take care of Marcus. Have him taken to his room, cleaned up, but do not tell King Idris until I return. As soon as you can find your mother. Tell her to ready herself for two injured men. Do not tell her it is your brother and Joe. Understand?" Yori asked as he threw a leg over his horse. Ezra nodded and watched his father and Samuel ride out of the stable. Samuel and Yori rode hard down the path Samuel sent their sons. Samuel wondered what had happened. The boys were only supposed to be ruffed up and scared. The blood on the saddles was evidence that much more went on. He swallowed a lump that rose up in his throat and looked at his brother. Yori would never forgive him if anything happened to Grayson. He had to convince Yori it was the wolves who hurt their children. After what had happened to Marcus it shouldn't be a hard sell. He worried of his own son's safety. All he wanted to do was for Joe to see it was in his best interest to break it off with Julie.

"There!" He heard Yori shout. Samuel looked ahead where Yori pointed. A body lie in the path on its side and as they rode closer, they could see there were arrow shafts holding the body in that position. Yori stopped his horse quickly dismounted and ran to his son. "Grayson!" Yori shouted. He assessed his son's wounds fearing he was already dead. He watched for his chest to rise with breath. It seemed like an eternity, but he saw him take one then another.

"Where is Joe?" Samuel asked with panic. There was a lot of blood, but his son was gone. A trail of where a body was dragged led away from the scene then disappeared. Samuel hurried back to where Yori was tending to his son. Taking his dagger, Yori broke the arrow tips and brought Grayson to a standing position.

"Grayson! Where is Joe?" Samuel asked shaking him to wake. Grayson's eyes fluttered. "Where is Joe?" Samuel's voice held panic.

"Dead." Grayson answered and his head fell against Yori's shoulder.

"Samuel." A voice called from behind. Samuel turned quickly and saw Seth, leader of the wolf nation standing there. "Your son is no longer of this world. I am sorry."

"If this is true where is his body. Show me!" Samuel

demanded with anger.

"I cannot. He was carried away by the wind. His body is no more. I was coming for the other boy when you arrived." Seth answered calmly.

"The other one is still alive! Was it your intensions to kill him as well?" Samuel shouted and drew his sword. A hundred wolves it seemed appeared out of the shadows. Their hackles stood and teeth bared ready to protect their king. A chill embraced his body as the sound of their warnings echoed around him.

"I did not kill your son Samuel." Seth walked forward unafraid.

"Like your son didn't kill Prince Marcus and his own sister, your daughter?" Samuel asked angerly.

"That was unfortunate, but your son was not killed by wolves as you well know. Your son's demise is a consequence of your own actions Samuel and no one else." Seth said quietly so only he could hear. Samuel's face revealed the truth behind Seth's accusation. "Get on your horse and leave. Go grieve the loss of your son as I will my daughter." Seth said walking away.

"Sam, let's go!" Yori shouted turning his horse around. Grayson faced his father in the saddle. Yori held him in place with one arm. His horse danced nervously in place as Yori held the reins tightly waiting on his brother. Samuel mounted his horse and turned the animal around to head back. He took a second and looked at the blood that soaked the ground. Knowing it was all that was left of his child. Grayson moaned against his father as they rode hard, his blood soaking into Yori's clothes. Clara was standing in the courtyard when Yori arrived. Yori slid out of the saddle with Grayson in his arms. Clara followed him up the stairs to their room. She grabbed her scissors and began cutting off her son's shirt.

"You did not send word I would be trying to save the life of my own son!" She looked out of the corner of her eyes.

"What good would have it done to cause you worry until now?" Yori said as they worked to remove his clothes.

"Where is Joe? Ezra said two would be coming." Clara asked as they removed the remaining shafts of the arrows.

"He didn't make it Clara." He paused. "There's more."

"As if this isn't enough?" She asked looking at her son. "Marcus was killed. Ezra found him in the wolf nation." Yori said helping her hold Grayson on his side.

"Does Idris and Lilly know yet?" Clara asked just as the bells tolled.

"They do now. Samuel must have told them." Yori shook his head.

"Barrett bring Mother that pan of water. Hurry now." She urged. "Yori go take care of the king. I will send Barrett to find you if…" She couldn't finish her sentence. She refused to speak the words.

"Clara, we've got to get Vada here to the safety of the castle. When Samuel and Idris start addressing the deaths of their sons, I'm afraid of what the outcome will be. We must protect her." Yori said heading toward the door. He took one last look at Grayson then left the room.

"He looks really bad, Mother. Is Grayson going to die?" Barrett asked handing her bandages.

"Well, we're not going to let him are we? Here press hard here and don't let up." She directed him to a wound that was spilling blood.

Grayson opened his eyes and focused on Clara. "Mother," He whispered. "It hurts to breath."
"I know son, it should ease soon." She wanted to cry for her son but couldn't let either boy see that she was worried.

"Mother…am I dying?" He asked pushing blood out of his

mouth. She brushed the hair away from his face and smiled.

"That will be up to you and how hard you fight." Clara said kissing him on the forehead.

"Don't give up Gray. I promise I will give you all my biscuits." Barrett begged. Grayson managed a slight smile and then closed his eyes. Barrett looked at his mother with fear.

"He's just resting. Let's finish up the bandaging so he can start working on getting better, ok?" Clara reassured Barrett.

******

Yori walked in on Samuel and Idris in an angry session which was exactly what he had feared.

"Your Majesty, I am very sorry for your loss." Yori bowed respectfully.
Idris nodded to Yori. "Any news of Grayson?"

"It is not good." Yori said his jaw clenching. Idris sat on his throne gripping the chair arms with force, the knuckles on his hands turning white. Samuel was feeding the king's anger with plots and sceems to take their revenge. The grief of his own son overshadowing his senses.

"No, you're allowing your pain to dictate your decisions. You can't justify the annihilation of a whole kingdom of people over one man's mistakes. It is delusional." Yori pounded the table beside him.

"Says the man whose son still lives." Idris mocked with anger.

"Your Majesty," Charles stood up and walked over by Yori. "We must investigate this further before talking of war. Demand that Seth brings Austin in to face his charges."

"What of Joe, Charles? Who will answer for his death?" Samuel shouted.

"Problems with the wolf community started with your father." Idris said to Yori. "My father had to deal with his indiscretions that conceived Jack if I need to remind you. All that has now passed onto me and I have inherited a problem that has proven to be on ongoing threat that has been ignored way to long." King Idris stood. The memory of his wife's heartbroken tears and wails of pain tugged at his heart. "We grieve for our sons when we should not. I will not let this happen again." Yori and Charles glanced at each other. They didn't like where this was going.

"Please, my lord King let us tackle this when cooler heads and painless hearts prevail." Yori pleaded.

"I agree with Yori my Lord, a pause to grieve for the boys then we shall gather for council once again on this matter." Charles said walking over to stand next to Yori.

"I see your wisdom gentlemen." Idris sighed. "However, how weak would I seem if I sat and waited because of feelings? No, I think swift retaliation is the answer."

"Sam, I am saddened with the loss of my nephew, but you must see this is not the answer. Punishing a whole kingdom of people for one's mistakes is barbaric." Yori said turning toward his brother.

"It's not just one's mistake this is colossal and Yori they are animals, scoundrels, mutts if you will, not people." Samuel bit back at his brother. He wanted revenge and he wanted it now. He would find the man he paid, and he would die.

"Samuel burn them! Set their fields on fire!" King Idris ordered.
"Your Majesty, I implore you to wait." Yori stepped between him and his vision of Sam. "Have I misled you, my Lord?"

"No, Yori you have not but your way is a peaceful solution

that sits ill with my stomach." Idris said bitterly. "My orders stand, Yori. Everyone leave me." He waved them away.

"Samuel, we must delay this order. He's not thinking straight." Charles said after leaving the room.

"Why? Because he wants revenge for his son?" Samuel said stomping off.

"We've got to get Vada somewhere safe." Yori said quietly.

"If we can't stop this crazy plan, we must make sure the wolf princess is safe. We promised her father when she was born." Charles reminded.

******

"Where is your mother?" Yori asked Barrett when he entered their suite.

"Lady Sara called her away to the Queen's side." Barrett answered sitting next to Grayson not taking his eyes off his brother.

"Barrett, what are you doing?" Yori asked sitting down in a chair by Grayson.

"Mother told me not to take my eyes off him. I am to watch each breath and if something changes, I am to run to her." Barrett said continuing to stare at Grayson's chest. "But Father I really need to pee." Barrett started to squirm in his seat.

Yori laughed. "I will watch him in your stead while you go."

Barrett looked at his father with squinted eyes. "Sware you will."

"I promise, Barrett, go!" Yori nodded watching him hurry out the door. Yori sat up on the bed and looked over his son. His face was so pale. He looked close to death. "I am here son." Yori spoke to Grayson. He smiled briefly remembering the day he was born. He was so small and fit in the palms of his hands.

Grayson moved his arm and moaned waking himself. "Father I am thirsty."

"Sure son." Yori took the cup at his bedside and helped his sit to drink. "Don't drink too much it might leak out all those holes."

Grayson smiled at his father's humor and was still struggling to breathe. "My arm hurts."

"It is broken, Grayson. Try to be still." Yori spoke calmly.

"Father," Grayson started to cry. "Joe, he was drowning in his own blood." Grayson's voice was wheezy. "It was horrible. Father, he begged me to…I didn't want to do it."

"Grayson, son his death would have been worse to have drowned. You did the right thing." Yori tried to console him as Grayson cried out with grief. Yori wiped the blood away from the side of mouth that trickled out.

"I'm going to be sick." Grayson said rolling to the side of the bed with Yori's help.

Barrett came in as Grayson started puking. "What did you do, Father?"

"Barrett, go get your mother, now!" Yori shouted. Blood seeped through the bandages as his wounds reopened.

"Hang in there Gray, you've just got too much blood in your belly." Yori explained. Clara rushed in gathering her skirts and climbing onto the bed behind Grayson. She put pressure on the bleeding wounds and he cried out from the pain.
"Yori, you will have to help me set his arm. I cannot by myself." Clara told her husband. When they rolled Grayson back over Ezra laid his head against the doorframe when he heard his brother scream out in pain

as they set his arm. He couldn't go in. Instead, he turned and headed to the arena. When he arrived, it was with rage. He jerked off his shirt and pulled his sword.

"Who will spare with me?!" Ezra shouted. He twisted the sword around at his side. Walking in circles around the arena he shouted again. "Come on! Spare with me!" There was pain echoing in his words.

"I will spare with you, Ezra." Charles said pulling his blade from its sheath. They circled the arena a couple of rounds before Ezra swung his blade, then he continued to swing at Charles with all the pent up hurt and anger he was feeling. Charles blocked his blows but did not give Ezra any ground. "Pull strength from your anger. Use it, do not let it control you. If you let it cloud your mind, Ezra you will die." Charles coached and stopped with his blade at Ezra's throat. Ezra yelled swinging his sword around knocking Charles blade away. "Ezra! Stop!" Charles stuck his sword in the ground. "Take a minute." He smacked Ezra. "Do as I say. Close your eyes and take a deep breath. Now, all that anger and hurt you are feeling, channel all that emotion into your blade. Until you learn to direct that energy you will always be a good swordsman, but you will never be a great one." Ezra opened his eyes and listened to Charles. "Now let's try it again." Charles said pulling his sword from the ground. Ezra's swings became smoother as he focused on transferring his energy. "Much better, Ezra." Charles nodded. When they finished

Charles said. "Now that's how you fight!" He chuckled out of breath. "Remember being full of anger in battle could cause you to lose your head metaphorically and realistically." Charles squeezed Ezra's shoulder. "I've never seen anyone that has the talent that you do at such a young age. But don't let that go to your head, Ezra."

"Thank you." Ezra smiled with a slight nod of respect. Ezra picked up his shirt and when he looked up Asia and Vada were walking by with Lady Marcy. Asia smiled at Ezra admiring his handsome features. He threw his sword over his wide shoulder and flexed his chest muscles.

"Young ladies do not gawk, Asia." Marcy advised, then she whispered to the girls. "But a fruitful glance never hurt anyone." She nudged Asia with her elbow and giggled. "Vada, Lady Clara has asked for your help with her son, Grayson, who was attacked today." She said as they climbed the stairs.

Vada looked at Asia and then back to Marcy. "Yes, my Lady."

"Asia you will be attending to the Queen's needs as she is bedridden after hearing the news of her Marcus." Marcy said with sadness.

"Yes, my Lady." Asia answered her smile fading. They had all grown up together and her heart broke thinking these boys who were as brothers were gone. Marcy knocked at the door and heard Clara invite them in.

"Vada, I am so glad you are here." Clara said exhausted. Vada looked at Grayson lying on the bed seemingly asleep his chest and belly covered with bandages. Little spots of blood that seeped through the bandages marked where the arrows had entered his body.

"How is he doing, Clara?" Marcy asked giving her a hug.

"It's touch and go. It's been a battle. He throws up then his wounds will bleed." She said putting her hands on her hips. She was covered in her son's blood. It was even in her hair.

"Clara he is sleeping now let Vada sit with him and you get yourself cleaned up and take a nap." Marcy ordered her friend.

"Yes, I think I will." Clara let out a sigh and brushed her hair away from her face.

"Asia, have you seen Ezra? I haven't seen him at all today. He hasn't come by to see Grayson yet." Clara asked walking around to the other side of the bed where she stood.
"Yes, my Lady, he was in the courtyard with Lord Charles just moments ago." Asia said, trying hard not to smile as

she remembered how he looked in the arena.

"Come along Asia." Marcy said, turning away to leave and looked back at Clara after opening the door. "Clara take some time and rest."

"I promise." Clara raised her hand. "Ok Vada, sweetheart." She said after Marcy and Asia closed the door. "I will be in the next room if you need me. Watch for fever and wake me if he worsens."

"I will." Vada said and waited for her to leave the room before sitting beside him. She bit her lower lip as she looked him over. He looked terrible she thought. She reached for his hand, hesitated then decided that 's what she wanted. She raised up his hand and rubbed it across her cheek. A nice sensation filled her body. She kissed the top of his hand and then laid it back on the bed. Before she could pull her hand away, he caught her fingers. Her eyes flew up to meet his. Grayson didn't speak but managed to smile.

"Hello." She said smiling back at him. His eyes fluttered and he was asleep again. The door opened and Barrett stood in the doorway staring at Vada.

"Who are you?" Barrett asked as if he was aggravated she was there.

"I am Vada. Your mother is resting and asked me to watch over your brother. Is that ok?" Vada asked amused by his attitude.

"I guess so." Barrett climbed up on the bed and laid down by his brother. "Are you going to be Grayson's girlfriend?" Barrett asked crossing his arms over his chest.

"Maybe, if he asks me to. Would you approve?" Vada asked as he yawned.

He shrugged. "Your pretty. Yes, I think it would be ok." Barrett rubbed his hands together. "Would you read me a book?"

"I do happen to have one with me." She pulled the book out of her satchel and read the title to him. "It's about a boy who befriends a bear."

"Well, that would be crazy. Everyone knows that bears are cranky." Barrett informed her. "But you can read it anyway." Vada smiled and began reading it to him. Before she was finished, she looked up to see he was asleep. But Grayson wasn't. She blushed when she made eye contact with him.

"I thought I was dreaming." Grayson whispered with a slight smile.

"Would you like a drink?" She asked when he touched his throat and he nodded to her question.

"My mother?" He asked after taking a sip.

"She is resting in the next room." Vada answered quietly.

"That's good. You look beautiful." Grayson said his throat raw from throwing up. "I am glad you are here." He took her hand in his.

"Me too." She smiled. "I was hoping to see you just not like this." She added quickly. Yori heard voices in his room and cracked the door slightly. Vada giggled after something Grayson had said to her and it made Yori smile. He peeked in the room and saw Grayson holding her hand. Barrett was sleeping beside his brother. Yori rattled the door to give them notice he was entering.

"Grayson, bud it's good to see you awake." Yori said standing at the foot of the bed.

"Father this is Vada." Grayson introduced.

"Vada, nice to meet you." Yori nodded.

"You as well, my Lord." She bowed her head.

"It looks like you're in good hands here. I've got some

issues to put to bed then I'll be back for the night." Yori said patting Grayson's foot.

He started to leave when Grayson called for him. "Father." Yori turned to see that Grayson was getting sick again.

"Hold his stomach tightly, Vada." Yori said as he turned him over. Clara heard him from the other room and hurried to help.

"It hurts." Grayson cried between bouts of puking.

"I know son." Clara said feeling helpless. Barrett woke and jumped off the bed. He ran to his room and covered up his head crying.

"My arm." He said as he rolled onto his back. Clara placed a rolled blanket under his arm lifting it up level with his body. Vada feeling a wet feeling on her hand looked down to see it covered in Grayson's blood. She looked at his bandages to see they were soaked with.

"Vada grab that basket there with the bandages. We will need to change these." Vada did as Clara asked and helped her with the task at hand. Yori answered the knock that came at the door.

"Father." Ezra said and glanced at the chaotic scene around his brother. "Father there's fire all around the wolf nation. Charles is waiting for you at the stables. Can I go?"

"No, Ezra, I need you here." Yori said looking back at Grayson. "If something happens to Grayson while I'm gone your mother will need you." Yori said softly placing his hand on Ezra's shoulder.

Fear struck Ezra. "Is it possible?"

"Yes, it is. You have not been here to see that he struggles. It wouldn't hurt for him to know you are here." Yori said walking away. Ezra watched his father hurry down the hall then looked back at Grayson. Clara saw him in the doorway and walked over to him. She was wiping blood from her hands onto her apron.

"Ezra, I have worried about you all day." Clara said to her oldest.

"I am sorry Mother. It has been a trying day." He looked past her to Grayson. "Father said Grayson's injuries are serious."

"Yes, Ezra they are. It is up to your brother to fight." She looked over at Grayson to see Vada was washing his face with a cool cloth. "I know you have had a horrible day, son. What can I do to help."

"Mother this cannot be fixed with bandages and medicine. It's just something I must figure out on my own." Ezra said looking down at the floor.

"Still, I have an ear and open arms, Ezra and bandages can metaphorically be applied to wounds of the heart." Clara took Ezra's arm and urged him inside. "Would you sit with him for a few. I need to check on the Queen." Clara asked, untying her apron and laying it on the bed.

"Vada is here." He said nodding at her.

"Please Ezra." Clara pleaded. He gave in, nodding his head. Ezra gave Vada half a smile and plopped down in the chair beside the bed.

******

Charles had both horses saddled and ready when Yori entered the stables.

"Idris ordered Samuel to set fire to all the homes and buildings in the wolf nation. He said and I quote 'Let them all burn' " Charles said as Yori mounted his horse.

"We had better get there fast then." Yori said and urged his horse quickly out of the courtyard. The villages were engulfed in flames when they arrived. Women could be heard screaming and crying for their children. Scorched and burning wolves were littering the ground. Children covered in soot were standing screaming out for their parents. The air was full of stench and smoke. The carnage was exponential. Yori pulled his kerchief around his mouth and nose while they searched for Sameul.

"There! Yori." Charles pointed through the smoke.

"Samuel stop!" Yori yelled over the collapse of someone's home as the fire overtook the structure. They heard Samuel yell and another round of arrows carrying fire lit up the sky. "Samuel! Yori shouted again. Samuel looked at Yori and Charles and rode in their direction. "Samuel this is madness!" Yori yelled in disgust.

"These people are innocents." Charles growled.

"People? They are not human. Heathens maybe, animals, but not people." Sameul snarled. "Yori, these are the king's orders." He grinned at his brother. Samuel turned his horse around to return to his men then looked over his shoulder. "Stand with me brother or stay out of my way." Samuel kicked up his horse heading back.

"He's lost his mind." Charles said unbelieving.

"Let's see who we can help." Yori said dismounting. He grabbed his shield to protect himself from another round of arrows that Samuel may unleash.

******

"Why are you acting like this?" Vada asked Ezra watching him pout. "Your brother could die, and you are behaving as a child."

"I would rather be somewhere else, Vada. I should be finding Austin and bringing him in to stand trial. I should be out there looking for whoever shot Grayson and killed Joe. I can't sit here and watch my brother die." Ezra said angrily kicking the underside of the bed.

"Grayson's going to die?" Barrett's little voice cried. Vada looked at Ezra with anger. He dropped his head in shame.

"Come here Barrett." Ezra said regretting his tone. "I think Grayson's too ornery to die, don't you?"

"Ya he is." Barrett smiled and climbed up on the bed next to Grayson. Barrett kissed Grayson on the cheek. "I love you bubby. Get better please." Barrett looked at Ezra and rubbed his belly. "Ezra, I'm hungry."

Vada stood and held out her hand to Barrett. "Come on, Barrett let's go to the kitchen. I'm sure we'll find something good there." She gave Ezra a side glance. "I'm sure Ezra will watch over his brother for a while."

"Vada, I know nothing about tending wounds." Ezra panicked.

"He's sleeping, Ezra, I'll be back before he wakes. You'll be alright." Vada assured him leaving the room with Barrett. Ezra stood and walked to the window. He wondered what was going on with the fire. He wished his father would have let him go instead of making him stay with his brother. He turned and looked at Grayson. Why did Samuel really send them on the northern path? It was hard to believe that the wolf people would have wanted to kill Grayson and Joe. But after what they did to Markus and Angelina he wasn't sure. A light knock on the door brought him back from his thoughts. It was Asia.

"Hi Ezra, Vada said you were here alone with Grayson, so I thought I would check in." Asia said smiling.

"I am glad you are here." Ezra smiled back walking over to her.

She put her hand up to stop him. "I am afraid you are mistaken Ezra I am not here to see you." He looked at her with confusion. "I am checking on Grayson and Vada told me about what you said in front of Barrett."

"I didn't know he was there, Asia." Ezra said in his own defense. "Is that really what your mad about or are you still ill-tempered that we stole your clothes." Ezra winked at her and sat in the chair by Grayson that was opposite of Asia.

"Yes, to both!" She snapped and she wanted to stay mad but that dimple that pops when he smiles at her makes it very difficult to remain so. "You and Grayson got Vada and me in a lot of trouble with my mother." Asia said shaking her finger at him.

"Come over here and I'll make it up to you." Ezra said patting his lap for her to sit.

"You think it's going to be that easy for you?" She asked as she felt Grayson's temperature. "Ezra he's burning up." She said alarmed. Asia uncovered his chest to check the wounds. "Ezra go get your mother." She said as she dropped a washcloth in water and wrang it out. Ezra left quickly and met Vada in the hall with Barrett.

"What's wrong?" Vada asked seeing the urgency in his face.

"He has fever. Asia has sent me to get my mother." Ezra said as he passed by her. Vada gathered her skirts and with Barrett hurried to Grayson.

******

A maid came out of the Queens room as Ezra arrived. "Would you be so kind as to call Lady Clara. I am her son. Tell her it is about my brother." Ezra asked the young girl.

"I know who you are, Lord." She smiled with a curtsey and hurried back inside the Queen's room. Clara immediately followed the girl out with a quickened pace.

"What is it, Ezra?" Clara asked concerned.

"Asia sent me for you. Grayson has fever." Ezra said and watched his mother step back inside and quickly return.

"I was fearful this might happen." She said as they hurried back to Grayson. Asia was continuing to cool him down with wet cloths when they entered the room.

"My Lady, one of the wounds looks bad." Asia said as she lowered the bandage.

"Vada, in that drawer is some salve. Please apply it to all his wounds." Clara said as she tried to stir Grayson.

"Grayson, son wake up, let's drink some water." Ezra, I need you to raise him up." Ezra removed his sword and climbed onto the bed to help. "Gray, open your eyes, sweetheart." Clara pleaded.

He didn't open his eyes but spoke to her. "Mother, I don't feel well."

"I know, son, drink some water it will help." She said with an easy motherly tone. Ezra looked at the women in the room and how exhausted they were. Suddenly, his desire to elsewhere be was replaced with shame. He looked down at Grayson and feared, really feared he might actually die.

"Gray, open your eyes brother." Ezra whispered. Then he said something that no one else could hear and a faint smiled Grayson's lips. Clara held the cup up to his mouth and he drank. He opened his eyes then and searched the room until he located Vada. She blushed and lowered her head at the way he looked at her. Clara saw the connection between her son and Vada was growing.

"Vada come and help him drink." She waved her over to her side of the bed. Clara pretended to fuss with the blankets and bandages. "Keep the cool cloths on his skin and try to get him to drink as much as he can." She started to walk into the next room to check on Barrett then turned at the doorway and looked back. "Ladies, your mother is having a room set up for you next door for the night. She will be staying with the Queen." Grayson settled into sleep again and Vada sat down in the chair pulling a blanket over herself. Asia yawned standing by the window.

"Asia why don't you get some rest. He will probably sleep the night." Vada said watching her eyes close.

"Come on Asia I will walk with you." Ezra offered and she accepted. He held her hand until they reached her door and he opened it for her. "I hope you sleep well Asia." Ezra kissed her cheek. He waited until she was inside and told her good night as he closed the door. She stood looking at the closed door from her side confused that he didn't insist on coming in. Asia opened it expecting him to be standing there waiting on her, but he wasn't.

"Ezra." She called his name. He turned to look at her but did not walk in her direction. "Are you alright?" She asked concerned.

"Yes, just humbled." He smiled with saddened eyes.

"Ezra." Asia walked up to him and took his hand leading him into her room. She unbuckled his sword and carefully laid it across the chair. "There is no one here but me. Time for you to grieve." Asia pulled him close to her, but he pulled away.

"I am fine." He said rubbing the back of his neck.

"How can you be fine? You have lost your best friend, your cousin, and possible your brother all in one day." She said softly touching the side of his face. "Will you let me be there for you?"

He chuckled. "When you say it out loud it does sound awful." He lowered his head. "I don't want you to see me cry." A rouge tear escaped, and he quickly batted it away. Asia blew out the light and pulled his hand to the bed. They lay there together, and Ezra cuddled up close. Asia held him while he cried.

"I love you, Ezra." She whispered to him, her heart breaking.

"I love you too, Asia." He said to her and realized in that moment he meant it.

******

Grayson woke to darkness except for the moonlight that shone through the window. It gave him enough light to see that Vada lay beside him in the bed. He needed to pee and was reminded of his injuries when he moved to get up. His stomach was very tender. Holding his middle he slowly rose to relieve himself. There was a cup of water at his bedside, and he drank all of it. He went to the window just to stretch and realized he felt better. He looked back at the girl in the bed and smiled. Her long black braid lay across her chest and rose and fell with each breath. Absolutely beautiful, he thought to himself. Slowly, he made his way back to the bed snuggling up close to her. He put his arm around her waist and rested his head next to hers. Vada laid her arm on top of his and they both drifted back to sleep.

******

Yori made his way up the candle lit stairway to his residence in the castle. Snatching up one of the candles he opened the door to his suite. He wasn't quite sure what he would find when he entered but his son cuddled up to a girl in his bed was not it. Quietly, he walked into the adjoining room where he found Clara asleep with Barrett. She awoke when his boot hit the floor.

"Yori?" Clara asked raising up slightly.

"Aye, I would ask about Grayson but since his arms are around Vada in our bed, I'll assume he's better. Clara couldn't tell if Yori was humored or irritated.

"He had a fever today; it must have broken." She said as Yori lifted Barrett and put him in the other bed in the room. "What happened, Yori?" She asked as he slipped in bed next to her.

"Idris ordered Samuel to burn the wolf nation to the ground. By the time Charles and I arrived there wasn't much left. We did what we could to get the survivors to the cabin in the woods. It was horrible Clara. I never would have thought Idris could be so cruel." Yori was still in disbelief at the atrocity.

"Did Samuel do nothing to stop it?" Clara asked.

"No, Sam is so eat up with his own hurt and anger he fed right into it." He kissed her forehead when she turned toward him and put her arm over his chest.

"What of Vada's inheritance?" Clara asked fearful.

"Everything and everyone linked to her is gone. The only ones left that know about her being wolf and now Queen since her family is gone, is our group. As long as she wears the ambulant, she is safe." Yori yawned hugging her.

"I hope we are doing the right thing with her, Yori." Clara worried.

"Me too." He answered. "But I am afraid things are going

to get far worse my dear."

******

Asia woke feeling Ezra shift to lay on his side. She was now face to face with him. This was the first time they had spent the night together. She really liked it and lay there listening to him breathe. His features were so handsome. Asia smiled to herself when she remembered the perfume she hijacked from her mother's dresser drawer. Quietly, she got up and went through her bag. "There you are." She whispered and dabbed a bit of it on the back of her ears, between her breasts and just below her belly button. Climbing back into bed she snuggled up next to him. He moved his arm over her waist and feeling that she was naked his eyes popped open. She heard him inhale and waited. Ezra wiggled closer to her sniffing her ear.

"What intoxicating scent do you wear that stirs my blood, Asia?" He asked kissing her jawline.

"I stole it from my mother's things." She giggled. "Do you like it?"

"What do you think?" He asked when he moved his hips to hers and she felt him swollen against her. Ezra followed the trail of the potion that led between her breasts. "You are but a witch casting spells upon me, woman." He pulled her underneath him and continued kissing her down the path of the perfume. Asia squirmed as he reached the end of his journey. She grabbed his hair with her fingers and pulled him back up to face her. "What Asia? Tis your fault I am wanting." When she arched her breasts upward, he smelled her again. Ezra buried his face in between them and then drove her mad with desire when he kissed each one individually. The smell of that hypnotizing perfume was the undoing of his resistance and when she reached between them touching his member, he lost control.

******

Grayson stood at the window staring out watching the people preparing for the life celebration of their beloved prince. Food was being prepared and the aroma had filtered upward and tickled his nose.

"Good morning son." Yori said coming from the adjoining room buckling his sword. "It is good to see you up on your feet." Yori smiled with relief.

"How are you this morning, Grayson?" Clara asked gently hugging her son.
"I am hungry, Mother." He replied with his hand on his

stomach. Vada stirred and was embarrassed that she had been caught waking in the bed of a man's parents she barely knew. Grayson walked over to the bed taking her hands when she stood. He kissed her cheek. "Thank you, Vada, for keeping me warm." Grayson told her then looked at his parents. "I became chilled during the night."

Yori raised his eyebrow at his son. "Uh huh, well, in any case I will be taking my own bed back tonight."

"Come along Vada we shall freshen up before breakfast." Clara insisted taking her hand and leading her away. Vada looked back at Grayson with fear in her eyes.

"Nothing happened, Father." Grayson said hoping his mother wasn't angry. "That's the one you should be worried about." Grayson said of Ezra when he ran inside and locked the door behind him. He had his boots and sword in one hand and trying to hold his pants up with the other. He looked up at his father and Grayson as he sat to pull on his boots.

"Morning!" Ezra said a smile spreading across his face.

"Are you running from Asia's mother again?" Grayson asked.

He chuckled. "She told me if I planted a babe in her daughter, she was cutting it off and throwing it to the dogs." He laughed again. "She was very angry." He said pulling his shirt over his head.

"Ezra, what am I going to do with you?" Yori asked smacking him on the back side of the head.

"What?! We weren't doing anything until she put on that perfume. Once she did that all bets were off." Ezra shook his head remembering the smell.

"Yori chuckled rubbing his chin. "I don't know where those women got that perfume, but your mother was wearing it the other day and..." Yori said with a smile that made the boys throw up their hands to stop him from talking.

"No! Father please." Grayson pleaded. Yori laughed as he went to the door to answer a knock.

"The King has requested your presence in the throne room Lord." A messenger stated.

"Come on Ezra, you had better stay away from Asia today, and your mother for that matter. After Lady Sara fills her ear of you bedding her daughter, she'll be grabbing the strap." Yori said as Ezra walked out in front of his father. "Grayson take the day to rest and regain your strength. I will talk to you later, son." Yori said and closed the door. Clara came back out with a shirt for Grayson and helped him put it on.

"Mother, I hope you didn't say anything to Vada. She's a sweet girl. We really didn't do anything." He said as he sat on the bed holding his belly. She helped him with his boots then looked up at him. She patted his leg.

"I believe you son, and I said nothing to her about it." She stood and held out her hands to him. "Come on, let's have some breakfast. Vada!" she called to her. When Vada entered the room, Grayson's mouth fell open. Clara put her fingers on the bottom of his chin and closed his mouth with a giggle. Vada's hair was braided to the side and she was wearing a pretty dark blue dress with soft lace embellishing the sleeves that hung at the elbows. Vada had Barrett's hand and when he saw Grayson he shouted and ran to his brother.

"Hey Barrett." Grayson said and grunted when Barrett bumped his belly.

"I'm sorry, Gray." He looked like he was going to cry.

"It's all good Barrett. It's just tender. Are you hungry?" Grayson said then looked at Vada. "I know I am."

******

Yori sat at the table with Ezra listening to Samuel and Idris complain about the farmer's request for seed. When the squabbling continued he finally had enough and stood. Charles was standing on the opposite side leaning against a pillar and chuckled when he saw Yori rise. Samuel and Idris both stopped and looked at Yori.

"Do you have something to say brother?" Samuel asked with irritation.

"The farmers have a right to complain to you about their need for seed." Yori walked around the table and stood in front of Idris. "You destroyed their supply chain when you wiped out the wolf kingdom. The smaller farmers bartered with them and without that ability for trade those families are likely to lose their farms. They will then have to move into the city and then overcrowding begins." Idris and Samuel looked at him with surprise. "With one selfish act of retaliation you have changed the natural balance of our world." Yori could see Idris was starting to anger and he put up his hand. "I am not saying that Austin shouldn't have been reprimanded for his actions. I just think that the fallout would be less detrimental had a more level headed approach been made."

"You talk like a man who has not lost a son." Samuel whipped around to see his brother. "Had that been the case you probably would have done the same."

"I did not lose a son, but all were affected by it. Ezra is the one who found Marcus, your Majesty. Have you forgotten their friendship? Grayson has been a breath away from death since he was injured. But our personal losses and pain cannot blind up from making better decisions for the kingdom." Yori sighed. "My suggestion for the farmers is for the court to bear the burden for seed and supplies to be brought across the seas."

"Aye." Charles raised his hand. "This would indeed help, put us back on the right track until we can replace the resources on our own soil."

"The cost of the journey across the sea would drain the courts finances. I could impose a tax that would help us recover, but we are not a wealthy nation. We cannot do this without the people's help." Idris said standing from his throne and walked down the steps between the men.

"Perhaps, to raise the taxes a little would help. I'm sure the people could handle it for a while." Charles suggested.

"Yes, that is reasonable." Idris agreed. "Samuel tomorrow we shall address the people with this issue. Now all leave but Ezra and Yori." King Idris ordered and waited for the door to be closed. He turned to face Ezra. "Ezra, you have been a very good friend to my son since you boys were under foot." Idris managed a smile. "I am sorry I have not stopped to thank you."

Ezra bowed to Idris. "I loved him like a brother, my Lord." He said his voice quivering.

"I would like you to ride point at the ceremony in his honor." Idris said putting his hand on Ezra's shoulder.

"Thank you, your Majesty." Ezra answered, lowering his head.

"Now if you will excuse us your father and I need the room." Idris touched the side of Ezra's face as a father would his son. Maybe, Ezra thought in some way he felt like it was Marcus he touched. After Ezra left Idris turned and faced Yori his demeanor changed.

"It is obvious that my decision to attack the wolf nation was unjustified to you. How would I have looked to the people had I let them be with a slap on the wrist for the murder of the crowned prince? Weak! Pitiful and vulnerable!" Idris spat. I am hurt by your skepticism."

"It cost the lives of innocent people and children, my Lord King." Yori said calmly to his friend.

"They took my child from me!" Idris shouted. "My son!" He pounded his chest with his fist. There was so much pain in his heart he felt like he could barely breathe.

"I know Idris." Yori let him weep holding his friend closely.

******

Vada stayed with Grayson while the rest attended the celebration of life for Marcus. "I'm sure you had rather be with them then babysitting me." Grayson said as they walked slowly down the hallway together their arms linked. "I am fine."

"Yes, yes you are." Vada said looking at him out of the corner of her eyes.

He chuckled. "Where did that come from, my Lady? You have been quiet since you have been here watching over me."

"I wanted to see if I really liked you." She shrugged.

"You couldn't tell at the river?" He frowned. "I have to work on my skills, I guess."

Vada giggled remembering that day. "I wasn't referring to that. I love your spirit. I feel connected to you somehow." Grayson stopped at her room turning toward her and pinned her to the door. He placed his hand softly on the side of her face and kissed her. "Can you give me a moment?" She asked turning the knob behind her. He looked puzzled as she shut the door in his face. Quickly, she rummaged through Asia's things until she found the perfume. She dabbed a little behind her ears and carefully returned it. Grayson was leaning up against the wall opposite of her room waiting.

"Everything ok?" He asked smiling at her. That smile liquified her insides and those dimples of his set her on fire.

Um hm, yes." She answered tucking her hair behind her ear. He slipped his arm around her waist and continued to walk down the hall.

"I was wondering if you would like to walk with me to the market later?" Grayson asked and kissed the top of her head. That's when he caught a whiff of the perfume.

"I would love too." She giggled when he stopped her to sniff her earlobes.

"What are you doing?" She asked as he continued to breath her in. Now he knew what Ezra was talking about when he spoke of the perfume that Asia wore.

"You smell delicious." He growled as he nibbled her neck. They heard footsteps behind them and they walked further down to Grayson's room. Once inside he sat down in a chair and pulled her onto his lap. He grunted with pain when she landed, and she immediately jumped up.

"Oh, Grayson are you ok? I am sorry." He grinned at her when she put her hands on either side of her face in panic.

"No Vada I did it to myself. Please come and kiss me." He begged reaching for her hands. She gathered her skirts and straddled his lap.

"Is this ok?" She asked gently moving closer. He put his hands on her bottom and pulled her close enough he could feel her breasts against his chest. The aroma of her perfume attacked his senses again. Grayson left his hands on her bottom while they kissed.

"Vada, I don't think it is fair of you to be so beautiful and smell so inviting when I am unable to bed you." He said as he nuzzled her earlobe. "I know you can feel that I want you. I just don't think my wounds will allow the movement." She sat back and looked into his eyes.

"I am sorry Grayson, Asia told me to try it the next time we were alone I just didn't realize the perfume held such power." She stood up running her hand down his chest and across his lap.

"My dear Vada, the aroma of the perfume is but a compliment to your beauty." He said as she walked around behind him her fingertips trailing up his arm to his shoulders. She kissed the side of his face and his neck. "I do not need it to desire you."

"But it is a nice embellishment?" She asked as she ran her fingers through his soft black hair.

"Tis." He turned his head to look up at her. "We will have to try it again when I can enjoy you better." She smiled contented and began to braid his hair. He allowed her to shave the sides of his head leaving the braided top. She hummed a tune while she gently played with his hair and it relaxed him enough he began to nod off.

"Grayson, why don't you nap? I'll come back later for our walk." She kissed his cheek.

"I think I will. Will you stay until I fall asleep?" Grayson asked as he laid down on the bed. She lay beside him holding his hand looking into his eyes until his closed and he began to lightly snore.

******

Idris stood in front of the kingdom to address the issues of taxes. "In order to compensate for our losses of trade with the wolf nation and the cost of traveling over the seas, a higher tax must be imposed. I am hoping that it is short lived and it can later be rescinded." Idris announced. Samuel and Yori stood on either side of the king and watched the reaction of the people as he made his speech.

"This is of your own making, your Majesty. Why must we suffer for your mistakes?" One said angrily.

"The wolf nation could not go without punishment for their crimes against the crown. The loss of Prince Marcus is felt by the kingdom and the world." Samuel barked back at him.

"The King has mentioned it is only a temporary solution. I think we can all handle it for a short time." Yori spoke up as Idris received news from Lilly's hand maiden and whispered to Samuel.

"You must excuse me; my wife is ill." King Idris said then left back inside the castle, Samuel following.

"Lord Yori." Another raised his hand. "What of us that have only small farms? A tax increase of any kind is devastating."

"Then maybe you could relinquish your farm to the crown avoiding all tax on your property." Prince Henry interceded walking up next to Yori. He stood like his father but did not carry the same presence as Idris or Marcus. Henry was a young man with a smaller frame. He almost had a weasel like appearance and wanted to try out his new position as the next in line to become king.

"Henry, do not speak for your father." Yori warned in a lower tone turning his head to the side.

"I am a Prince, lord Yori, do you forget my title and your place?" Henry replied in the same warning tone.

"I beg your forgiveness, Prince Henry, I implore you to consult with his Majesty before speaking on his behalf." Yori said and Henry nodded understanding.

"I feel my father to be grief stricken over my brother's death and very generous. This court has suffered because he is a king of good heart. You should not be so quick to show disloyalty." Henry finished and then looked Yori up and down. He left with his entitled nose in the air following his father.

"Bear with the royal family through this most difficult time. As for the seed, in order to have ample amounts we will have to sail overseas which is very costly. We all will have to endure a few hardships before it can get better." Yori said after hearing grumbling and arguments in the crowd.

"You know as well as we do that none of us can afford the taxes he speaks of. Even a collection of two months' time will seal our fates." A farmer shouted.

"Carl, I share your concerns. Give us some time to figure out a course of action that will benefit all of us. Go on home now. All of you." Yori said with frustration turning away from the farmers and townspeople.

******

Ezra met Yori in the hallway in passing and stopped him. "Father, do you have a moment?" Ezra pleaded. Yori looked down the hall. He was on his way to speak to Idris to talk to him about the taxes but when he saw the need in his son's face he stopped and smiled at Ezra.

"Yes, Ezra what can I help you with?" Yori asked.

"Father," Ezra shifted his feet and fiddled with the hilt of his sword.

"Are you alright Ezra?" Yori asked trying to be serious.

Ezra blew out a breath. "I want to ask Asia to marry me." There he thought it said aloud.

"Well," Yori scratched the side of his face. "I was wondering when you were going to get around to it. Do you have a ring?"

"No, I don't." Ezra answered his smile fading.

"Come with me." Yori said and headed to his room. He searched through a drawer and pulled out a linen sack. "Ahh here it is." He handed it to Ezra and he pulled a ring out of the bag and admired it's beauty. "It was my mother's." Yori smiled remembering it on her finger. "Have you asked her father?" Yori chuckled at the fear that crossed over Ezra's face.

"Father, Asia's mother wants to dismember me. If I go out there I might not come back." Ezra's face turned white.

Yori slapped his leg and laughed. "Maybe, but it's the right thing to do. You'll be alright. Do you love her?"

"I can't see my life without her." Ezra said looking at the ring again.

"Then you will ask her father." Yori said raising his eyebrows.

"Yes sir, but if I am not home for supper you'll know where to find my body." Ezra laughed nervously. Asia and Vada was standing on the balcony when they saw Ezra ride out of the courtyard in his dress coat and his sword on his back.

"I wonder where he is off too?" Asia asked.

"You love him don't you, Asia?" Vada asked smiling at Asia's blush.

"I really do." She said with a sigh propping her head up on her arms.

******

Ezra practiced his speech as he rode out to talk to Asia's father. Twice he stopped his horse and tried to reason with himself not to turn around. This particular trip was the longest ride to Lord Andrew's farm he had ever taken. When it was a trip to see Asia, he would ride quickly, anxious to see her. But this time was to see her father, to ask for her hand in marriage and it was a stressful journey. Asia's father was sitting on the porch smoking his pipe when he rode up.

"Ezra." He acknowledged him taking the pipe from his mouth.

"Lord Andrew, may I approach?" Ezra asked and dismounted his horse when Andrew nodded. When Ezra walked up the porch steps Andrew offered Ezra a seat.

"What can I do for you Ezra?" Andrew asked looking over his glasses at the young man. Ezra looked at his hands and rubbed them together nervously. Andrew smiled at the boy's hesitation.

"Sir I...I um. I love Asia." Ezra looked up respectfully when he spoke. "With your permission, Lord Andrew, I would like to ask for Asia's hand in marriage." Ezra said and let out a quiet sigh.

Andrew took a couple of draws from his pipe. "I was wondering when we were going to have this conversation, my boy. Are you planning to stay with the King's army?"

"Yes, my Lord I am committed to the crown." Ezra didn't know why he was so nervous. He and his father had had many conversations with Lord Andrew and he always felt at ease then.

"And you and Asia will continue to live in the castle?" Andrew asked.

"Yes, we will. I hope someday soon to possess lands of my own and raise my family there." Ezra said nodding hoping this conversation would wrap up. He had his dress coat on and was smoldering.

"Ezra, I have known you since you were a pup. Take off

your jacket and let's talk like the family we are. I am giving you permission to marry my daughter." Andrew said with an affectionate slap on Ezra's knee.

"Thank you, my Lord." Ezra grinned taking off his jacket. "I was burning up."

I appreciate the gesture and the respect you have shown me today. You have great presence, Ezra, who knows maybe you'll be a king someday." Andrew sat back in his chair and puffed on his pipe. They continued to visit about the issues involving the king and his actions with the wolf nation until late in the day.
"I had better take my leave before Lady Sara returns." Ezra said standing. "She's been upset with me of late."

"So, I have heard." Andrew chuckled shaking Ezra's hand.

******

"Samuel, I have decided to double the taxes. If we are to develop the lands of the wolf nation that now belongs to the crown, we will need the funds to do so." Idris said to Samuel in a private meeting.

"I agree, my Lord, instead of sending for seed and supplies abroad we can use the money here and increase the crowns' finances quickly. We could also, use the King's army to secure the trail to the northern border. Those lands will bring more wealth to his Majesty's purse." Samuel smiled leaning back in his chair. "And if your Majesty pleases, I could steward that land for him. A trusted advisor would be suited for such a position."

Idris looked at him and smiled. "Your thinking is of the left shoulder where evil sits Samuel. But it is pleasing to the ear." Idris rubbed his hands together. "We shall have to study more on this plan. I am disappointed in Yori's lack of support. We've all been a great team but his loyalties seem diminished and his mind elsewhere."

"His concerns are with Grayson, my Lord. The last word I have is that he isn't doing very well." Samuel said regarding Yori's lack of duties to the King.

"Ahh, yes that is probably so." Idris nodded. "I shall call on them soon."

"When do you want to tax collection to begin, my Lord?" Samuel asked redirecting King Idris's thoughts.

"Tomorrow, I want you to handle this personally Samuel. Do not bother Yori with this it will only create argument." Idris added rubbing his temples. "He is a great friend but can be very righteous." Idris stood, he was tired and ready to be alone with his wife. As he started to leave, he looked back at Samuel. "Take Henry he will enjoy taking the people's money."

******

Yori was lying across the bed when Clara entered the room. She tried to be quiet thinking he was asleep. He startled her when he spoke. "How is Lilly?"

"Weary of tears and carrying the babe." She said covering her heart with her hand then sat to take off her shoes. "Since my son is not abed, I am assuming he is better?" Yori asked his arm lying over his eyes.

"He and Vada took Barrett to the market for a walk." As for Ezra, I haven't seen him all day." She said letting down her hair.

"There is a good reason for that." Yori chuckled. He raised up on his elbows to see her reaction. "Sara caught him in bed with Asia this morning. She threatened to dismember him if he gave her a babe."

Clara's mouth flew open. "He's your son alright."

"What is that supposed to mean, Clara." He asked smiling.

"You were the same way at his age. Always trying to get under my skirts." She said as he pulled her to the bed with him.

"It didn't help that Asia got ahold of some of the perfume that you were wearing the other day." Yori said wrapping his arms around her.

"Oh, she didn't." Clara giggled.

"Yes, she did. So, she is just as much to blame for their fun." He kissed the top of her head. "Ezra rode out to talk with Andrew today."

"Oh, what about?" Clara asked and was hopeful of her son's intensions.

"Marrying his daughter." Yori smiled as she raised up to look at him.

"That's the best news I've heard in a while." Clara said and then thought of the advice that Marcy had given her and Lilly. A wicked smile crossed her face as she climbed on top of Yori's waist. He looked at her with surprise as she unbuttoned his pants. He raised up to touch her and she pushed him back down, wagging her finger at him. After freeing him she shifted her weight down his legs until she was in perfect position. Yori moaned out loud when he felt her mouth around him. He looked down at her and watched her and it made him want to explode.

"Clara, if you don't stop, I am going to…" He warned but she didn't stop. She continued with her oral torture until he released. "Woman I don't know where that came from but thank you." He said pulling her up into his arms.

******

Yori was sitting at his desk leaning back in his chair his arms crossed over his chest when Ezra knocked and entered. Ezra was puzzled at the bewildered look on his father's face. "What's on your mind father?" Ezra asked sitting on the corner of his desk.

Yori grinned and scratched his chin. "Something your mother did."

"By the look on your face, I'm going to guess that I don't want to know." Ezra closed his eyes shaking his head.

"Probably not." Yori laughed. "What's up son?"

"I want to take Asia out tomorrow and I was wondering if there was anything I needed to be here for?" Ezra asked kicking at the desk with his heel.

"Enjoy your day, Ezra. Oh, how did it go with Andrew?" Yori remembered.

"I came back with all my body parts intact so that's a plus. But yes, it went very well." He paused a moment and looked at his father like it just hit him. "I am getting married."

"That is if Asia agrees. You haven't asked her yet." Yori shrugged and chuckled at the frozen look on Ezra's face when he realized that she might not say yes.

"Do you think she won't agree?" He said with fear in his voice.

"Never assume anything." Yori teased.

Ezra touched his stomach. "Why is there so much anxiety for a man in these matters? I think I am going to be sick." Ezra ran from the room. Yori laughed and slapped the desk.

Barrett ran in after Ezra left and crawled up in his lap. "Did you have a fun afternoon?"

"Mmhum, Grayson bought me candy." Barrett said pulling a handful out of his pocket. "A pig got loose and was running through the market. The man was trying to catch it and fell down." Barrett slapped his knee laughing. Barrett stopped laughing and froze. He started shaking with fear not able to speak.

"Barrett, what's wrong?" Yori asked seeing the fear in his son's face. Barrett pointed at his father's desk then buried his face into Yori's shoulder. "What Barrett? I don't see it." Yori tried to pry his son from him, but his grip was strong.

"Monster on your desk! Mother! Mother! He cried which brought Clara sailing in from the other room. She saw the fear on her son's face and the confused look on Yori's.

"Is there a spider somewhere?" Clara asked calmly. She had seen Barrett react this way before when he saw a spider drop from the ceiling. Yori examined his desktop and found a tiny spider sitting by his paperwork. "He is very scared of them Yori." Clara said taking Barrett from his father.

"How are you supposed to slay a mighty dragon if you are afraid of a tiny spider?" Yori asked with a frown.

"I can slay it as long as he doesn't have those." Barrett shivered. "Monsters on it." He turned away from Yori and looked at his mother. "Can we move now?" Tears welded up in his eyes.

"Alright Barrett you've had a long day. I do believe it's time for bed." Clara said taking him to his room.

Grayson knocked on the door then stepped in. "Are you ok son?" Yori stood noting that he looked ill.

"I think I pushed it too far today, father." Grayson said looking down at his shirt that was soaked with his blood.

"I would say you did." Yori said helping him off with his shirt. "The wing still tender?" He asked when Grayson grimaced with the movement of his arm.

"Very." Grayson grunted.

"Clara!" Yori shouted at his wife. He took the scissors and cut the bandages away from the wounds. Grabbing some more he placed it on the one that was bleeding telling Grayson to hold pressure. Clara came around the corner to see Yori sitting Grayson down in the chair. She brought the salve over and applied it to his wounds.

"It stinks, Mother." Grayson said turning his head away.

"Yes, but it works. No walks tomorrow. Stay in and rest, understand?" She looked at Grayson sternly.

"As long as Vada can be my nurse." He grinned winking at her.

"Grayson." She warned.

He chuckled at her. "I am very tired. I think I will go to bed." He said after she bandaged him.

******

Prince Henry rode out with Samuel and some of the guards the next morning. He sat tall in his saddle feeling important and empowered. Samuel looked at him and shook his head. He thought he looked pompous and arrogant. He didn't want to deal with the prince's self-righteous attempt to convince him that he would be the next in line to the throne. Lord Andrew was standing on his porch when they rode up to his farm.

"Lord Andrew we are here to collect the taxes you owe the crown." Henry said looking at Andrew with entitlement.

"Samuel, I have already paid my taxes. What is this all about?" Andrew said stepping off his porch.

"My father, King Idris, has issued..." Henry said hatefully but was interrupted by Andrew.

"I know who your father is Henry." Andrew spat.

"Arrest this man!" Henry shouted to the guards. When they started forward Samuel put up his hand to stop them.

"Lord Andrew, you will address the prince with his inherited title." Samuel rolled his eyes.

"My apologies, Prince Henry, my temper is short from an already heated morning. May I inquire the reasoning behind the extra taxes?" Andrew bowed his head.

"In order to restore the lands newly acquired taxes must come from the people. Everyone must contribute Lord Andrew." Henry informed with sanctimony. "We will return in two days for your share." He urged his horse forward with the guards close behind. Samuel stayed back to talk to Andrew.

"Sam this is not going to work. Small farms cannot withstand such taxes." Andrew scowled.

"Things will get tougher before they get better, Andrew you know that." Samuel said.

"Not if that little whelp succeeds in becoming king." Andrew shook his head.

"Can't disagree with you there." Samuel agreed leaving and catching up with Henry.

******

Ezra woke early remembering his plans for the day. He was both excited and nervous. He hopped up and froze when he saw Vada curled up next to his brother in the bed across the room. Luckily, she was still sleeping and didn't get an eye full of his morning salute. He pulled his pants on quickly just in case his movements woke them. He would dress casual today but wore his tall riding boots. After his stomach had settled last night, he shaped up his beard, braided it, then shaved the back of his head to ear level. The rest he pulled back and tied up. Ezra looked back at his brother, walked over to his side and watched for breaths.

"Ezra, what are you doing?" Grayson asked his eyes still closed.

"Good, you're awake." Ezra kneeled beside him. "Did you know that there is a girl in your bed?"

"Yes." Grayson opened his eyes and looked at Ezra. "What's up Ezra?"

"I am asking Asia to marry me today." Ezra said with a smile spreading to cover his face.

"Congratulations, brother! That's great!" Grayson said with quiet excitement.

"Thanks, umm Gray do you think she might say no?" Ezra asked with his smile fading. Grayson turned toward Ezra and propped his head up with his hand.

"She will say yes, Ez. You should have no worries." Grayson assured his brother.

"Ok." Ezra blew out a nervous breath then stood. "I will see you tonight. Maybe we can all do something later, the four of us."

"Yes, sounds good. See you tonight." Grayson said as Ezra left the room. Grayson rolled toward Vada and hugged her closer. He kissed her cheek and went back to sleep.

******

Ezra knocked on Asia's door twice before she answered. "Good morning, Ezra." She smiled sleepily.

"Asia, I would like it very much if you would spend the day with me." Ezra asked and she noticed he seemed nervous. She smiled noticing that he had taken extra care to look good for her.

"Give me a few minutes to get ready." She said touching his beard admiring his handsome features.

"Meet me in the courtyard. I will saddle the horses." Ezra said and quickly kissed her lips.

"Ezra." She said as he walked away. "You look very handsome." She said and blew him a kiss. He all but skipped down the hall and rode the banister rail down to the kitchen level. The kitchen lady popped him with a towel when he hopped up on the counter.

"Get ye behind down from there Ezra!" She looked him up and down, noticing he had changed his appearance. She covered her mouth with her hand. "Is today the day? Being all spiffed up and handsome. I'd be figuring I am right." She winked at him. Ezra pulled the ring from his vest pocket and showed it to her. She gasped. "It tis so beautiful! She be a lucky girl, that one." She handed him a lunch he had requested yesterday. "I think I spied some flowers in a vase just outside the kitchen." She said and blushed when he kissed her cheek.

"Thank you! You are the best!" Ezra shouted as he snatched the flowers.

******

His father and Charles were saddling up for a ride when he entered the stables.

"Well, flowers and a lunch." Charles said grinning. "Thank you, Ezra."

"Sorry my Lord, but these are for someone much prettier than you." Ezra said pointing the flowers in his direction.

"Where are you riding to today?" Yori asked mounting his horse. "Just in case." He added when Ezra frowned.

"We are riding the river trail to that big field of her father's." Ezra said as he readied the horses.

"Keep your eyes open son." Yori advised as he and Charles rode out of the stables. Ezra was waiting on Asia in the courtyard with the flowers in hand. She had left her hair down and it was swaying back and forth at her bottom as she walked. She wore a very pretty dark purple dress and carried a parasol.

"You are beautiful." Ezra grinned and kissed her lips.

"I can't remember the last time I have seen you out of uniform, Ezra. You look very handsome." He handed her the flowers and then helped her on the horse. Ezra barley spoke as they rode and Asia noticed that his nervousness was still present. "Ezra, is there something wrong?" Asia asked with concern. He wasn't himself. Ezra was always lighthearted and calm. Today he was anything but that. "Ezra!" She shouted and he jumped. "Why are you on edge today?"

"I am sorry Asia. Too much on my mind I suppose." He said looking at her quickly then back at the road ahead.

"You invited me remember?" Asia asked with irritation. When he didn't reply she stopped her horse and turned it around to head back.

"What are you doing?" He asked surprised.

"You invited me out but you haven't spoken ten words since we left. If you are breaking up with me, I want to be going in the right direction." Tears were building up in her eyes and he felt horrible. Ezra hopped down and went to her side.

"Please Asia." He held his arms up to help her down. "It's not what it seems. I am not breaking up with you." He brought the horse back around and took her hand. She wouldn't budge when he tried to walk with her. "Tis not the place I wanted to do this, but you are forcing my hand."

"Well, I am not taking another step until you explain yourself." She stomped. It was not playing out like he had imagined. He tied the horses by the river then took both her hands in his.

"Asia, I have always known that I loved you. But the night we spent together showed my heart that I was truly in love with you," Ezra pulled the ring from his vest pocket and kneeled in front of her. She covered her mouth with her hands. "Will you marry me?" He asked her looking into her eyes.

"Yes! Ezra, yes, I will marry you." She waited for him to place the ring on her finger then jumped into his arms. "I am in love with you as well." Now there were tears of happiness welling up in those beautiful eyes.

"This ring belonged to my grandmother, now it will be worn by my wife." Ezra said as they looked at it together. The world seemed to have lifted its weight from his shoulders and he felt himself again.

"It is beautiful, Ezra. I am honored to wear it." She wrapped her arms around his neck and kissed him.

"I want to ride down farther there is something I want to show you." Ezra said picking her up in his arms and helping her back on her horse.

"I am sorry I messed up your plans, Ezra." She said ashamed of her anger.

"You didn't, it just happened a little sooner. Honestly, I am glad, the wait was killing me." After they made it back on the trail he yelled. "I asked and she said YES!!"

"Now there's my Ezra." She laughed. Then he started singing. Asia tried to be supportive, but he just couldn't sing. A dog barked and whined covering its head as they passed by. But she said not a word. He was very happy, and she just sang along with him.

******

When Grayson woke again Vada was staring at him. "Good morning, beautiful." He smiled kissing her lips. He could faintly smell the perfume from the night before and it aroused him. He pushed his hips against her so she could feel his swollen desire.

"Good morning to you too!" Vada said as she touched the side of his face with her hand and kissed him again. "Why is it that I feel so connected to you Grayson? Do you feel the same, or is it just me?" She asked between kisses.

"I too feel like our spirits are bonded." He smiled.

"Are you just saying that so you can get between my legs?" She asked with a devilish grin.

"It would be a lie if I said no, but I really feel there is something building between us." Grayson kissed her neck and nuzzled her protruding nipples. He pulled her gown over her head and threw it on the floor. He looked into her eyes for permission to continue and when she looked back at him with no fear he continued to kiss her. Carefully, he lifted himself on top of her testing the soreness of his stomach. His eyes locked onto hers as she wrapped her legs around his waist. He groaned, but it wasn't from pain. It was desire. She arched her body up to his, inviting him in. Grayson's hand went between their hips touching her as he kissed her lips. "Are you sure?" Grayson asked as her head tilted back.
"Yes!" She begged. "Please Grayson." His fingers found her and she rose to meet them. Her breasts rubbed against his chest igniting a fire within him that burned with unrelenting intensity. Her eyes widened when he entered her.

"Are you ok?" He asked as she bit her lip looking uncomfortable. "Do you want me to stop?"

"No, Grayson I'm ok. Please do not stop." She pleaded and matched his movements.

"Vada, you feel so good wrapped around me." He whispered in her ear. "You are so beautiful." He kissed her lips. "Open your eyes, Vada, I want to see those black eyes when you reach your pleasure." She did as he asked and squeezed his shoulders when she exploded. The wild look in those eyes of hers sent him over the edge and he joined her in sweet release. They lay together kissing, touching and discovering. Slowly and tenderly, they made love again.

"I am hungry." Grayson said rubbing his belly. He felt something wet and looked down to see the troublesome wound had opened and was bleeding. "Uh oh," He said looking at Vada.

"I brought your mother's bandages with me last night just in case I would need them." Vada said slipping on her gown and grabbing what she needed. Vada quickly cut away the blood soaked bandage, applied the salve to the stubborn wound that was slow to heal then wrapped him with new clean bandages.

"I am going to sneak to my room and change. Will you pick me up on your way to breakfast?" She asked kissing him again. He pulled her back onto the bed and kissed her again. "Grayson, your mother will be checking on you soon. I must go." She giggled and walked to the door.

"Vada," He called to her as she opened the door. "Will you

be my girl?"

"Yes, Grayson, I will be your girl." Vada blew him a kiss and left the room.

******

Yori and Charles rode slowly and carefully to the cabin deep in the woods. The horses were nervous as they continued down the trail. Their ears were twitching, and they tried to turn back in the direction they had come from. Yori's horse snorted and sidestepped as brush popped beside them.

"Whoa, now." Yori rubbed the neck of his horse trying to calm him.

"They are all around us, Yori." Charles said stopping his horse.

"Yes, they are." Yori said stopping beside him. He looked behind but saw nothing.

"Yori, Charles, you will not be harmed." Seth said calmly, stepping into the path.

"Your wolves are scaring our horses. We've brought

supplies and I would hate to lose it because they can't behave." Yori said aggravated at having to keep his horse from bolting.

"Enough." Seth raised a hand to his wolves. "You are welcome, and I promise they will leave your animals be." Yori and Charles dismounted and followed Seth in the cabin. "Come inside."

"How are your injured?" Charles asked sitting at the table.

"Starting to heal. We have lost a few more from burn related infections." Seth said sipping on a cup of coffee his wife handed to him.

"We have brought salve and bandages with our supplies." Yori said and thanked her for the coffee when she handed it to him.

"Yori." Amanda said sitting by her husband. "What of Vada? How is she?"

Yori smiled and took a sip of his coffee. "Well, she has been tending to my son, Grayson, as he heals. I think they are starting to like one another."

"She still wears the ambulant?" Seth asks with concern.

"Yes, she does." Yori answered.

"I hope you can discourage that romance before it develops into something more. We've lost enough of our children over matters of the heart." Amanda said trying not to cry.

"What of Austin, Seth? Does he still live?" Charles asked bluntly.

Seth sat up straight and sighed. "Something happened to Austin after he took the lives of Marcus and his sister. He told Ezra that he acted with orders from me, but I told him no such thing. He told his mother that he had a vison that soon there will be a way for wolves and humans to become one. So, my son with some renegade wolves left our community to look for said way."

"Did he attack my son on the road to the northern borders?" Yori asked with concern.

"That was not done by wolves, Yori. That was brought about by your own people to make it seem like it was us. There are humans in the hierarchy of your government that would love to see us extinct." Seth said, crossing his arms over his chest.

"This is why it is crucial you keep Vada safe." Amanda said, refilling their cups. "My niece must also remain unaware of her lineage."

"She wears the ambulant binding her abilities to shift believing it was her mother's, so she never takes it off." Yori said sitting his cup on the table.

"What do you do next, Seth?" Charles asked, leaning back in his chair.

"We will stay here unless pushed out. We will grow strong again but stay quiet. If we can go unnoticed in the northern border, we can use its resources to survive." Seth stated patting Amanda's hand when she placed it on his shoulder.

"King Idris is adamant about using those lands to gain profit." Charles said.

"Samuel keeps chirping retribution in his ear keeping the wounds open and raw." Yori added. "My brother lost his last son; he has a right to be bitter but not at the expense of innocent lives."

"There is no way back from this, gentlemen. The Wolf nation and humans will never reach camaraderie again." Seth said with sadness.

"I hope you are wrong, Seth. Maybe someone will find a way to right this wrong." Yori said and finished his coffee.

"We should be getting back Yori before we are missed." Charles advised standing.

"I am sorry for your losses my friend." Yori extended his arm to Seth. "Please send word to us if we can assist with anything."

"Give Clara and Marcy our love." Amanda said hugging them both.

"Thank you for the supplies. Live well my friends." Seth said as Charles and Yori rode away.

******

"This is my father's land." Asia said with recognition. Ezra handed her the blanket and grabbed their lunch.

"For now." He smiled as they walked down to the river. He glanced back at the sword sheathed on his saddle, a constant companion he seldom parted with. The blade seemed to be an extension of himself. Today was for her and he would leave it be.

"What do you mean, Ezra?" She asked spreading out the blanket on the grass.

"This field and twenty acres north will be ours. I have made an agreement with your father to buy this land. We will build a house and raise our family here." Ezra said standing proudly with his arm around her waist. She hugged him tightly.

"Ezra, this has been the best day ever! Oh, I can't wait to marry you." She kissed him and twirled around laughing. Ezra grinned at her fun and how happy she was. He caught her when she became dizzy and almost fell.

"Maybe we should have our lunch." Ezra chuckled. They lay on the blanket after they ate planning out their house and the life they wanted to live. Ezra heard his horse snort and whinny. He stopped talking to listen. Sitting up he looked around. He didn't move.

"Asia, when I stand, I want you directly behind me." Slowly, he rose, reaching behind himself for Asia. As he glanced around, he saw they were surrounded by wolves. His hand instinctively went for his sword and sighed when he realized it was still on his saddle.

"Looking for this?" Austin asked Ezra as he came out of the shadows. He swung Ezra's sword around testing its weight. "Very nice. I may keep it." Ezra noticed the blood dripping from the mouths of the wolves and Austin's chin.

"It was my grandfather's." Ezra said and looked behind him to see how close the wolves were. "Did you eat my horse?" He asked causing Austin to laugh out loud.

"Yes, better him than you huh?" Austin asked balancing the blade.

"What do you want Austin?" Ezra asked with aggravation.

"All I wanted was to fill my belly on your animal but now I see something else I'm hungry for." He said pointing Ezra's sword at Asia. Ezra looked around at Asia. She was not afraid.

"Austin, Ezra and I are betrothed, and you are on our land!" Asia boldly stood at Ezra's side her arms stiff and chin lifted.

"She is right you are trespassing." Ezra smiled raising his eyebrows.

"Oh, she's feisty and beautiful. Makes me want to bed her right here." Austin said grabbing his crotch. Ezra lunged forward and the wolves moved in quickly growling and snapping their teeth with warning.

Austin wagged his finger at Ezra. "Not a good idea old friend."

"It seems to me you are always needing muscle to back you up Austin. Are you too afraid to fight man to man? Put your dogs on a leash and show me you can. Unless you are a coward." Ezra waved him forward.

Austin stuck Ezra's sword in the ground. "Do you think I am afraid to fight you, Ezra? With a blade, definitely. I am not deaf to the rumors of your skills. But we'll see about what you can bring with just your fists. First, get rid of that pig sticker in your boot."

Ezra pulled the dagger and handed it to Asia. "Now you, agree to keep your dogs back and Asia stays safe."

"My word as a gentleman." Austin bowed.

"Ezra, I don't like this. He never has fought fair." Asia whispered. He winked at her and walked closer to Austin.

"You've been wanting a piece of me for a long time haven't you, Ezra?" Austin asked then motioned to the wolves. As they rushed at Ezra, they transformed taking him captive. Ezra thrashed around to look for Asia. One of them held her around the waist.

"Austin, you coward, let her go! I knew you weren't going to play nice." Ezra said struggling to get free. The one holding Asia cried out when she threw her head back into his nose. As soon as he let her go, she ran but was caught again.

"Are you alright?" Austin asked sarcastically to the one Asia nailed in the face. He nodded holding his nose.
"Ezra, she's a spicy little thing." Austin walked over to her, grabbed her face and kissed her. Asia bit down on his lip. He laughed when he stepped back then punched the side of her face. She lost consciousness and they let her fall to the ground.

"Austin, I will glorify in taking your head." Ezra said with calmed anger.

Austin laughed, "Maybe," He walked around to look into the eyes of now his enemy. "Well, you are not in any position to take anyone's head are you." Austin said as he slammed a fist into Ezra's gut.

"Just let me know when your balls drop so we can fight like men." Ezra coughed recovering from the blow to his stomach. His comment earned him an uppercut to his jaw. Ezra rocked his mouth side to side but still smiled. Austin pelted Ezra with blows to the face and continued to beat him until he heard horses. Austin and the others changed into wolves as they ran into the woods.

Ezra pulled himself over to where Asia lay. "Asia, my love, are you ok?" Ezra said wiping the blood away from his nose and mouth. One of his eyes was already swollen shut with a deep cut over that eye. The blood stung as it seeped around his eyelid. He rolled her over to see a purple and black bruise on her cheek. She was still unconscious but alive. Ezra heard the horses ride up quickly to where they lay and heard his father's voice. His other eye was closing fast so he couldn't see anyone now. Ezra held Asia's hand tightly afraid to let her go and searched frantically for the knife he gave her earlier. Ezra wielded it around in every direction, unable to see who was approaching.

"Ezra, son put the knife down she's safe now you can let go of her." Yori said softly and took the blade from his hand. Yori looked over at Charles with concern for his son.

"Andrew is just a mile away. We can take them there." Charles said pulling Ezra's blade from the ground and stuck it in the sheath of his saddle. He scooped Asia up and mounted his horse with her.

"Father is Asia awake yet?" Ezra asked holding onto his father as they rode down the river trail.

"No, son but she will be ok." Yori answered as they rode slowly.

"They ate my horse." Ezra said disgusted. "I'm going to find him father." Ezra said and Yori felt his son's body fall limp behind him and caught him before he fell from the saddle. Andrew came out of the barn when he heard them ride up.

"Sara!" Andrew shouted as he took his daughter from Charles. "What happened?" He asked looking at her swollen face.

"They were attacked by Austin and his renegade wolves." Yori said as he slid from his saddle with Ezra. Sara held the door open while they carried their children inside.

"Jenna, bring me some water." Sara told her daughter as she came skipping into the room. Yori looked upon Ezra's face. He was hardly recognizable.

"Yori," Charles said and motioned him out of the room. "Let Sara work." Yori looked at his son once more before leaving the room. He joined Carles and Andrew on the porch.

Andrew lit his pipe. "When Marcus died, we lost the best successor Idris had. He would have been a good king. Now it's Henry, he will not make a good king. He will be a greedy man and sucks the life out of everything he touches." Andrew growled blowing out smoke.

"You have no liking for that boy at all do you?" Charles asked chuckling. Yori stared off into the distance thinking as the two of them bantered back and forth.

"Yori?" Charles called to his friend.

"Yori," Andrew tossed a pebble at Yori's foot. "What's on your mind?"

"Things are starting to get out of hand. I'm worried that the king's orders to destroy the wolf nation has unbalanced our world. Our children are being attacked and killed. I fear that it is going to get a lot worse, and I am not sure I am willing to let my family continue to pay the price." Yori said sitting on the railing of the porch.

"I don't think we are at the point of treason to the crown, Yori." Andrew slapped the arm of his chair and stood drawing on his pipe.

"No, but I think we should be prepared all the same. They have already doubled the taxes. It's going to be tough to overcome it." Yori said shaking his head.

"We've been through worse times." Charles shrugged.

"Yes, we have but I didn't have children back then. Look, I'm just thinking." Yori said walking inside to check on Ezra.

"He's awake for the moment." Sara said when Yori came inside the room.

He sat in the chair beside the bed. "Ezra, son, can you hear me?"

"Father," Ezra spoke cautiously, careful not to break open the cuts on his lips. "I am ready to go home." He grabbed his side as he rose from the bed grimacing from the pain.

"Not with those busted ribs. You are staying here a few days to recover." Yori told his son helping him lay back on the bed. "I will bring you a horse on my return."

"You're leaving?" Ezra said with a little fear in his voice.

"I have to get back to let your mother know or she'll be out looking for the both of us." Yori chuckled patting his son's leg.

"The outcome would have been different Father had he fought with honor." Ezra said. He didn't want to bring shame upon his father.

"I know son. I know. It's difficult to win when you are outnumbered twenty to one. Don't be so hard on yourself." Yori said with compassion.

"I will find him Father. He won't get away with hurting Asia." Ezra said through a clenched jaw.

"Well, so let's get you healed up first." Yori stood. "I'll be back soon." He rubbed the top of Ezra's head with affection. "I love you son."

"I love you too, Father." Ezra said and he heard Yori's footsteps as he walked away.

******

"I'm heading back. Clara will have my head if I'm not back soon. I am sure Idris is suspicious of our whereabouts the last couple of days." Yori shook Andrew's hand. "I appreciate you looking after my boy. I will return in a couple of days with Ezra a horse."

"He can stay as long as he wants and needs too. He's going to be my family soon as well. Don't worry about a horse. I've got one here he can have. That black stallion out there needs a young strong hand to tame him." Andrew said as he stood and walked with them to the stables. "Trust me he will earn it." Andrew chuckled. As Yori and Charles mounted their horses Andrew patted the underneath of Yori's horse. "Yori, if it gets to the point that you fear, my family and I will follow you."

"Thank you, my friend. I just hope I am wrong." Yori looked down at his friend. Andrew stepped back out of the way and let them ride out.

******

Yori found Idris, Samuel and Henry in the map room. A map of the northern region lay spread out on the King's desk. Idris glanced up as they walked into the room.

"Well, I was beginning to consider you a deserter of the crown." Idris said without smiling and looked back at the map.

"My apologies, my Lord." Yori said with a slight bow and started to continue when Henry popped off.

"Apologies? You abandon my father, the King when he needs you the most and all he gets is an apology?" Henry said standing with his hands on his hips and his nose in the air.

"As I was saying," Yori said looking at Henry then back to Idris. "Ezra and Asia were attacked today." He had Idris's attention now.

"Are they alright?" Samuel asked standing.

"Ezra is busted up and Asia was knocked unconscious, but they will heal." Yori answered Samuel. "There were renegade wolves, my King, on lord Andrew's land." He said to Idris leaning up against the door frame. "It was Austin and some others that survived the fire. They are responsible for part of the raids." Then he looked back at his brother. "But not all. He did not kill Joe."

"How can you be sure?" Samuel snapped.

"The information comes from a reliable source that's how." Yori barked back at Samuel.

"Those who took Joe's life will be found. We will get to the bottom of it. As for Austin I want his head. You will find him and bring him back to face execution. This road," Idris ran his finger over the map. "I want secured. Since you don't have our sons to join you, you will have to pull your resources and pick from my army those best skilled for this quest." Idris looking at Yori and Samuel.

"What of me Father? Will I be considered for this journey?" Henry interrupted.

"Henry, you have no fighting skills what so ever." Idris said turning to face his son.

"I can shout orders as well as any." Henry rebutted.

"What you would do is get good men killed because they would be protecting you. No, you will stay here." Idris raised his voice with Henry embarrassing him. He stormed out of the room slamming the door behind him.

Idris looked at Yori. "Ezra's service will be missed while he heals."

"Thank you, my Lord. Will you be joining us tomorrow?" Yori asked Idris as he walked back to the door.

"Yes, I think I shall." Idris said after a moment of consideration. "Good day gentlemen." Idris said excusing them from the room. They bowed slightly to him then left. Samuel didn't speak to Yori but walked away leaving him standing.

"Sam." Yori called. Samuel stopped and turned but did not walk back to his brother. "What can I do to help you?"

"What can you do to help me?" Samuel mocked. "Try bringing back my son. Can you do that for me, brother? Because that is the only thing anyone can do for me. I can't even lay him to rest. I cannot say goodbye." Samuel slapped the side of his hip looking up with a sigh. He started to speak again then decided against it and walked away. Yori watched his brother until he was out of sight. His heart broke for his brother, and he knew it had to be hard for Samuel to look upon his living nephews and not feel anger. Yori walked over to the balcony that overlooked the courtyard. He saw Grayson standing by the arena watching the current sparing. He just stood with his arms crossed and didn't notice when Yori walked up next to him.

Gently, Yori slapped Grayson on the shoulder startling him.

"Father." Grayson acknowledged him.

"Have you been in there?" Yori asked gesturing to the arena.

"I picked up a blade and it felt like a burden of immeasurable weight. I don't think I will ever wield another one." Grayson said thinking of Joe.

"Maybe in time, son." Yori said understanding his pain.

"To say that I will leaves a bitterness upon my tongue, Father. I have no desire to carry another." Grayson said and walked away.

"Grayson, Ezra and Asia were ambushed today by Austin and his pack." Yori said as he walked in Grayson's direction.

"Are they ok?" Grayson asked turning around quickly.

"Your brother was severely beaten, and Asia was knocked out. She has a black eye and a cut on her cheek where Austin hit her." Yori said as they both walked back to the castle.

"Austin is a coward. He relies solely on the brute strength of others he controls. Do you want me to find him?" Grayson asked.

No, I have something else in mind. Do you think you can ride?" Yori asked as they walked into the kitchen. He had missed a meal and was hungry. There was bread on the counter, so he grabbed a piece.

"I think so as long as I don't have to ride hard." Grayson said rubbing his stomach.

"Tomorrow the King wants to travel the Northern Pass. He wants to end the raids and make the route available for travel. I need my best archer in the shadows. I have a feeling that those who attacked you and Joe will be watching. If they had an opportunity to eliminate the King, I believe they would do so. I have said nothing to anyone about you being in the shadows watching our backs. I think it is better that way." Yori handed a piece of the bread to Grayson, but he waved it away. "I haven't told your mother about Ezra. I had better get up there. We'll be leaving at first light."

******

Ezra woke and eased into a sitting position. He fumbled around trying to find his boots. He had to get outside before his bladder exploded. He couldn't tell if it was daylight yet or not, his eyes were still too swollen. Knocking something over he woke Asia from her sleep.

"Ezra? Are you ok?" She asked lighting the lamp beside the bed. She gasped when she saw the injuries to his face.

"That bad huh?" Ezra chuckled.

"What do you need, my love?" Asia avoided answering his question. His face was very swollen and there wasn't a place untouched by black and blue bruises.

"Is it daylight?" He asked trying to open his eyes.

"No, it is around midnight or so I believe." She answered.

"Are you ok?" He reached for her, and she took his hands. He touched her face and she winched when he bumped her cheek. Ezra jerked his hands back. "I am so sorry my "love that I couldn't protect you from being hurt. I have failed you." Ezra took her hands kissing them gently.

"Ezra you were being held down there wasn't any way for you to get away." Asia said softly. He wrapped his side with his arm to support his ribs. "You should lay back down.

"I need to go outside." He said searching for his boots.

"Here," She said and helped him with his boots. She crossed her arms over his knees and propped her head upon them.

Ezra placed his hands at the sides of her head. "What is wrong Asia? Do you change your mind of marriage? Am I now too ugly for you?" Ezra teased.

"Oh Ezra. No, too all your questions." She laughed. "I just love being with you. I don't want to wait very long to be your wife. I feel as though I already am."

"I feel the same, Asia. We could get married here on the farm." Ezra suggested as they stood.

"You don't want to get married in the castle?" She asked surprised. She led him out of the room and made their way outside careful to be quiet.

"Is that something you want? I don't care where it happens sweetheart as long as it happens." He smiled through painful lips. "Point me in a direction that I am not peeing on your mother's flowers." Asia giggled after turning him away from the house. She stood behind him and put her arms around his waist careful not to bump his ribs.

"I love you so much, Asia." He said when he turned back around to face her.

"I love you more." She challenged and guided him toward the porch swing. "It's a nice night do you care to sit with me on the swing?" She helped him ease onto the seat of the swing and then laid her head in his lap. He played with her hair and leaned his head back.

"This is nice." Ezra said relaxing. He took her hand and placed it on his heart. "This is for you and you only."

"And mine is for you, Ezra." She said, placing his hand on her heart. She sat up and climbed carefully into his lap. She touched a spot on his lips that didn't seem to have a cut. "Does it hurt here?"

"No, not there." He answered and she kissed that spot.

"And here?" She asked when she touched his ear.

"No, not there." He answered now smiling at her game. She kissed him on his ear and asked about his neck and kissed him there. "You might need to stop kissing me, Asia. I don't think it would be a good idea to take you on your parents front porch." He laughed.

"Probably not, but I want you all the same." She said and touched him feeling his swollen member and unbuttoned his pants.

"Do you not fear for the life of your betrothed?" Ezra asked and had to control a moan that escaped when she freed his shaft. She raised her gown up to her waist and eased down on him. "I guess not." He gasped as she rocked her hips against him. Quickly he covered her mouth when she cried out. "Your mother has already threatened to cut it off and feed it to the dogs and you are squealing loud enough to wake her. I would like to keep my manhood thank you very much."

"I am sorry." She whispered and looked through the window to see if anyone was walking their way. "We are good I think." Asia said as she rose up and down on him.

Ezra found her breast and nibbled it with his teeth. He wrapped his hands around her bottom and pulled her hard onto him. As he felt around her, he touched the spot that drove her crazy and rubbed it gently. She bit her lip hard as she felt herself explode. He followed her right after with his own release. He held her afterwards and they rocked in the swing together until falling asleep together. Andrew found them there the next morning cuddled up together.

"Asia." He woke his daughter. "Your mother needs your help in the house." When she rose, it stirred Ezra. He blinked several times focusing on his surroundings. He found Asia's face and smiled then frowned when he saw her bruise. Ezra gently touched her face.

"I earned it, remember?" Asia smiled and tugged on his beard. She left him to find her mother.

"Since the swelling has gone down enough you can see I want you to come with me." Andrew said, stepping off the porch. Ezra slowly rose from the swing and followed Andrew. They walked to the stables and the riding arena. A black stallion with high spirits galloped around in the circle. Its black mane was long and tangled. His eyes were wild and strong of will.

"I acquired him in a trade a few days ago. Sara wasn't happy with the arrangement, but I just had a feeling and followed through with it. Now, I am glad I did." Andrew said as they watched the animal dance around the arena. He looked at Ezra and how the young man lit up at the sight of the horse. "He is yours." Andrew added and grinned when Ezra whipped his head toward Andrew.

"Mine?" Ezra asked looking back at the horse.

"Don't get too excited. He's a very spirited animal. It's going to take a lot of work." Andrew said as he knocked out the old tobacco from his pipe on the fence post.

"Thank you, my Lord. I am forever grateful." Ezra said with his hand over his heart. "How can I repay your kindness."

"Just take care of my daughter." He said. "That's all I need." Andrew walked into the tack room and Ezra followed.

"I found your saddle. It needs to be cleaned. Between that and training the stallion should be good work for you while you heal." Ezra touched the saddle looking at the dried blood from his horse.

"I see you found my sword." Ezra said pulling it out of it scabbard. He looked it over and tested the point of it with his fingers. "I left it on my saddle because I wanted the day to be about Asia. I wanted it to be special. But I guess I should have kept it as arms reach at least." Ezra explained sliding the blade back in its sheath.

"Do you see me carrying a sword? I too am of the King's army least you forget. I wear no weapon on this farm. This is my peace, and no one will steal that from me. To lay down your blade to find your own peace with my child is an honorable man to me." Andrew smiled squeezing Ezra's shoulder.

"Papa! Papa!" Jenna shouted as she skipped in. "Mother says it's time to eat." Then she turned to Ezra. "Ezra, will you be my brother when you marry Asia?" She asked taking his hand.

"Yes, Jenna I suppose I will. Is that ok with you?" Ezra asked smiling down at her.

"I guess so." She said and ran back to the house ahead of them.

******

Grayson stayed back out of sight until his father, King Idris and his brigade rode out of the courtyard. Vada rode up next to him and handed him the reins to his horse. He hesitated before mounting remembering the last time he rode was when Joe died. He sighed and adjusted the quiver on his back. Vada understood his pause and said nothing waiting patiently for him to lead. Domminick, a trusted friend to Ezra, caught up to them just before they started down the trail behind the king. Grayson stopped after following them for about a mile.

"We should separate here." Grayson nodded at Dom.

"Stay safe my friends." Domminick said as he turned his horse toward the trees. Vada and Grayson rode in the opposite direction. Slowly they continued deep into the forest disappearing into the shadows.

******

"Looks like we have some company." Seth said stepping behind a tree as King Idris rode by.

"What is your plan, my Lord?" One of his wolves asked quietly.

"Well, I think I will just walk out and have a polite conversation with their King." Seth smiled at the young wolf. He transformed and ran ahead of the party. King Idris and his army stopped when the large black wolf walked casually into the middle of the path. Yori held his hand down to the side of his leg with his palm facing back. It didn't go unnoticed by Samuel, but he said nothing of it, yet.

Seth morphed to man and bowed respectfully to King Idris. "Good day, lord King."

"And to you." Idris returned the greeting.

"What business do you seek with his Majesty?" Samuel growled unhappy that their journey was halted. He was a little worried about Seth's intentions, since it was he who had acted on the King's orders to destroy the wolf's nation.

"Well, lord Samuel it was not you to whom I was addressing." Seth grinned at Samuels obvious displeasure. Seth turned his attention to Idris. "With all due respect, your Majesty, what are you and your men doing out here?"

"I owe you no explanations as to the business within my own kingdom." Idris shrugged and urged his horse forward. Seth growled at his animal and it backed up despite Idris's demands.

"You diidn't seem to think you owed an explanation for your business when you entered my kingdom and murdered my people either." Seth looked at the ground and took a deep breath calming his anger. "My apologies for my outburst. There are raiders down the road who await your arrival."

"That is why we are here, to make this passage safe for travel." Idris said impatient to be done with this interruption.

"Do we have your support?" Yori asked knowing full well the answer.

Seth laughed. "My support?" His face showed no humor. "No, the warning you have just received is all my clan is willing to do. If you die on your journey, then you die. We will neither support your cause nor contribute to theirs."

"Then step away so we may be on our way." Idris ordered.

"What is happening to you Idris? We used to be friends and brothers in arms. We followed your father to the ends of the earth."

"Until Jack..." Idris started to say.

"Jack!" Seth spat. "I am sick of his name. He is the excuse for every time there is trouble between our races." Seth threw up his hands. "My child died too, Idris. My son is lost to me." Idris did not reply to him but forced his horse around leading his men forward. Seth stopped Yori's horse and let it smell his hand. It didn't like the carnivorous smell of his blood and jerked its head back.

"Are you aware that Vada rides with Grayson?" Seth asked. Yori whipped his head around in the general direction of Grayson.

"No, I was not." He said frowning looking back at Seth.

"I will watch over them." Seth said and Yori nodded his thanks as he rode on.

******

"Well, he knows you're here." Grayson said seeing the look on his father's face. "And he's not happy." Looking at Vada he smiled. "Let's ride ahead a little bit. If there is a raid ahead maybe we can spot them first." Grayson said as they rode past them, Grayson whistled to let his father know their position. Yori glanced up the hillside as they rode between the trees.

Samuel swung his horse alongside Yori. "Why does Grayson follow?"

"To cover our backs Sam. If these are the same group that attacked the boys we're going to need his help." Samuel huffed, making his disapproval obvious. Yori looked at his brother and laid his forearm over the saddle horn. "Why are you so bitter toward my son?"

Samuel sighed. "He looks just like him, our father. I guess I've let my feelings of him transfer to Grayson unintentionally, I assure you." Samuel gave his brother a bit of a smile and returned to the king's side.

"You didn't believe any of that did you?" Charles asked riding up next to Yori.

"Not in the least." Yori smirked.

******

"It's a girl, Lilly!" Clara said as the babe arrived. She lay her next to her mother and they all gathered around to admire the baby. They feared Lilly would only get a few moments with her daughter. She had lost a lot of blood and having suffered with the incurable sickness they didn't expect her to survive and have more than a few moments with her child. Lilly looked surprised when she looked upon her daughter.

"Idris wanted a son, but secretly I wanted a girl." Lilly touched her tiny features and then glanced down at the foot of her bed. Lilly smiled and nodded her head.

"Lilly, who do you see?" Sara asked looking in the same direction.

"Marcus, my son has come for me." Lilly whispered. She no longer had the strength to speak aloud. "Ladies, you have been wonderful friends to me. I shall miss you." She looked at her babe one last time. "I love you sweet girl. Mother is sorry she must leave you." She kissed her little nose then took her last breath.

"Oh, Lilly." Sara said and covered her face with her hands. Clara stiffened her back and swatted a tear away that had escaped her eye. She picked up the babe and handed her to Marcy.

"Marcy find a nurse maid and take them to the nursery. Sara, you must send a messenger to find the King. Ladies we must keep the Queen's death to ourselves until his Majesty arrives. I will clean Lilly and have her ready." Clara looked at her friends, tears staining their cheeks. "Let's take a moment to gather our composure and act like nothing has changed but the birth of the Princess." Clara said her lip trembling. They looked at each other in silence, the only sound was the grunting of the hungry babe.

******

A man fell from a tree in front of Idris as they continued down the path. Sam raised his hand for all to stop and rode up to the dead raider. Charles and Yori stood guard at the King's side. Another dead man fell from the tree opposite the first with an arrow through his temple. Yori motioned for the barrage to encircle them. Samuel dismounted and rolled the first man over. He recognized him as the one he had paid to scare Joe and Grayson. There was an arrow through his heart. Sam spit on him and got back on his horse. Yori looked up on the ridge and for a moment saw Grayson and Vada ride through the trees.

Idris saw them as well. "Yori, always my strategist. I see your archers." An arrow struck the road beside Yori's horse. He looked up at the ridge and saw Grayson, sitting on his horse waiting.

"I'll be back, your majesty." Yori said and rode up to meet his son.

"There are about twenty men camped out about a mile head, ready to ambush." Grayson said when his father approached. "We could take most of them if you want. Dom is on the other side waiting for the signal."

"Grayson, why did you bring Vada? Have you taken leave of your senses?" Yori said angrily, looking from Grayson to Vada.

"You said you needed your best archer. She, is your best archer, Father." Grayson said nodding toward Vada. Yori was not happy, and he made no effort to hide it. "I am not understanding your anger." Grayson said confused.

Yori drew in a deep breath and audibly expelled it. "Take out what you can. We will give you a few minutes then ride in fast." Yori finished and rode quickly down the hill. "Grayson said there are approximately twenty men ahead waiting for us. The archers will ride ahead and take out as many as possible before we arrive." Yori explained. Sam led the barrage quietly and slowly down the path until they heard screams of dying raiders as they were struck by the king's archers. Sam looked back at the king who nodded his permission to enter the battle. Idris pulled his sword and yelled as they rode into the fight. Charles and Yori stayed close to the king as they fought the raiders. Idris, being a skilled swordsman, had no problem defeating each opponent that faced him. He smiled with each strike he made against them leaving a path of blood and death in his wake. Yori turned as a marauder, with the intentions of placing an axe in his skull, fell to his death from an arrow that flew from the trees. Vada had just saved his life. Glancing up he saw her standing with her bow readied with another arrow. Yori looked in the direction she was aiming, and it was at a man running toward the king with a spear. She let lose her arrow and the outlaw fell, his face skidding across the path, an arrow through the back of his neck. She looked at Yori and he nodded his thanks. She disappeared into the trees meeting up with Grayson. Samuel shoved his blade through another one's mouth as he ran upon him. He looked around for Idris. He found him crossing swords in a battle that could have ended sooner but the King was toying with his opponent. Samuel strolled up beside him and stuck the tip of his blade into the earth.

"Your majesty does this skirmish amuse you?" Samuel asked as he rested his hands on the top of his pommel.

"Actually, I am becoming rather bored." Idris said and stuck his blade into the chest of his challenger. Yori's archers drove the rest of the marauders into the swords of King Idris's men, finishing the battle. Yori looked around at the men lying dead on the ground as the soil soaked up their blood. Samuel saw the sadness in his brother's face regarding all the lives that had ended this day.

"It is a battle that was necessary to ensure the safety of others traveling this pathway, Yori." Idris said cleaning his blade in the grass. He had also seen the remorse in the face of his friend.

"It is never a celebrated victory for me when so many lives are lost." Yori retorted. A shrill whistle from the hillside caught his attention. He looked up to see Grayson pointing down the path. A rider was coming in fast. Charles and Samuel stepped in front of Idris with their swords readied to protect the king. Yori walked out into the middle of the path to greet the rider. He recognized the young man as a messenger of the court.

"What is your business?" Yori asked as he took the horse's reins when the horse stopped beside him.

"I have a message for King Idris." The young man said looking in the king's direction. Idris heard him and walked up to the messenger.

"What is your message?" Idris asked his first fear was that it was word of Lilly and the babe. His fear would be confirmed.

"The Queen has delivered, your majesty. That is the message I was told to give you." He said and hung his head to avoid eye contact with the king.

"You know more though, don't you?" Samuel said walking up behind the king.

"I only know rumors, lord." He said keeping his head down.

"Out with them!" Samuel shouted with irritation. The messenger jumped almost falling out of his saddle.

"I am not sure of the truth of them, but the news is not good. The staff whispers of the Queen's demise." The young man said shaking with fear.

King Idris ran to his horse. "I must get back." He said as rode up next to Samuel and Yori.

"I will bring the rest back, Yori." Charles said mounting his horse. "You and Sam get the king back safely." Grayson and Vada rode down from the hillside to meet Charles. Domminick joined them.

"What happened that they left in a hurry?" Domminick asked looking down the path.

"There is trouble with the Queen and the babe. That is all I know." Charles replied shrugging his shoulders. "Are you kids heading back with us?"

"Vada and I are riding to Lord Andrew's farm to see Ezra and Asia." Grayson said and then gestured to Domminick. "Are you riding with us?"

"No, I will be heading back with Lord Charles. He might get lost and will need a young warrior to help him find his way." Dom said snickering.

Charles looked at him and shook his head. "Boy, I'll show you lost."

"Safe journey to you." Grayson said as he turned his horse away from the group.

"Vada," Charles stopped her. "You saved the king's life today. Well done."

"Thank you, lord." She smiled and then followed Grayson into the woods.

"They seem suited for one another." Charles noted.

"I know he is pretty sweet on her." Dom said as they started down the path back home.

******

Idris stood at the door of his bedchamber while Sam and Yori removed his armor and chainmail.

"I don't know how to do this without her. She's my balance and my peace. If she's gone my heart has traveled with her for, I shall never love another." Idris said with a heavy heart.

"Do you want us to go with you, my lord?" Sam asked.

Idris placed a hand on the knob of the door. "No, I must take this journey alone." He nodded to his friends and then walked inside closing the door behind him. Clara sat inside at the foot of Lilly's bed and stood when the king entered. She curtsied deeply. Idris looked at Clara with hope, but it was shattered when her tears fell once again. His eyes drifted to Lilly and he rubbed the back of his neck and his face hoping he was dreaming.

"I will take my leave now, my lord and let you have your time." She said with a gentle bow of her head.

"Clara, she looks beautiful and peaceful, thank you." He said and after she left the room, he sat in the chair next to the bed staring at his wife. "I am sorry I was not here to say goodbye, my love." He gently caressed the top of her hand. "I remember the first time I met you. There was not the smallest amount of bashfulness in that tiny body of yours." Idris chuckled as he recalled the memory. "You walked right up to me and planted a kiss on my lips. You told me that we would wed and there wasn't anything I could do about it." Tears crept up in his eyes as the memories invaded his thoughts and heart. "Lilly, my precious little firecracker, I hope you are with our son on the other side planning for the day that I join you." He stood up and kissed her forehead. A tear dropped from his cheek onto hers and he gently wiped it away. Idris walked to the door and turned to take one last look at his wife before leaving the room.

He cleared his throat before speaking to Samuel. "Bring Henry to say goodbye to his mother then the bells may toll for her majesty." Idris looked down at the floor. "She shall lay by our son Marcus."

"She saw him, your son, before she passed. He came for her. I hope in some small way that is comfort for you." Clara said trying not to cry.

"It is, thank you Clara. Will you show me my babe?" Idris spoke with sadness. His daughter was asleep in her crib when they entered the nursery. He looked down at her then at Clara.

"You have a daughter, my lord." Clara smiled. A slight smile crossed his lips as he picked up the infant.

"She wanted a daughter." Idris said taking her tiny hand from under the blanket. She wrapped her fingers around her father's thumb with a tight grip. It humored him. "We shall call her Freya. That is what Lilly had picked out for her." Idris kissed his daughter on the cheek.

"She favors you." Clara noted.

"Let's hope not." Idris grinned. "Clara, do you mind giving me and the princess a moment?"

"Lilly loved you dearly, Idris." Clara said as she opened the door.

"I know." He answered then looked at this precious life he held in his arms. "What am I supposed to do with you Freya? Your mother should be here to skill you in the ways and duties of a princess." Freya started to fuss and gnawed on her fist. "Even as a babe you are born with the abilities to complain to men about things we in nature cannot fix." She became inconsolable and upon hearing the babe cry the nursemaid entered and took Freya from his arms. Idris stood and watched his daughter nurse. His heart felt as though it was splitting in half, and he felt sick and suffocated as he thought of his life without Lilly. He had to leave the room. He made it to the balcony where Yori found him with a tight grip on the edge. He was rocking back and forth trying to regain control. "It hurts to the point a blade could give remedy." Idris said looking over at Yori as tears uncontrollably flowed from his eyes.

"I am not giving you my sword to fall upon my friend." Yori said holding Idris as he wept. The bells began to toll for the loss of their beloved Queen Lilly.

******

Yori found Jack's cell in the farthest corridors of the dudgeon. He heard his brother singing and laughing as he approached his cell. Jack shielded his eyes from the torch that Yori carried.

"Hello Yori." Jack said in a chilling tone. Yori looked his brother over as he slowly walked over to the cell door.

"Are you eating Jack? You look like you've lost weight." Yori noticed his hollow cheeks and how his clothes seem to hang loosely on his body. Jack pounced at the door and laughed at Yori's reaction. He rocked his head back and forth in a comforting rhythm.

"I eat the meals send to me and then the meals eat me." He laughed. "Meal worms, roaches, maggots squirming around in my food. Sometimes I just let them have it. Then the rats find it and it becomes a game! Who wins? I say the rats! They eat the bugs and the garbage and at night when I sleep...they eat me." Jack raised his head to look Yori in the eyes. His eyes were a brilliant blue and seemed to glow. He sniffed the air and smiled. His fangs extended past his lips, and he ran his tongue over the tips of them. "Yori, you brought me food?"

"I did! Bug free." Yori smiled at his little brother. Jack snatched the sandwich away from him and put his back to Yori as he ate. "Are you having trouble controlling your wolf, Jack? Your fangs are longer it seems?" Yori asked as Jack devoured his meal.

"What does it matter? I am locked away in the dark. Does my mother's gift annoy you brother?" Jack asked turning back around grasping the bars pressing his head hard against it.

"Not at all. I am only concerned for my brother." Yori said and touched Jack's fingers.

"Don't touch me." Jack pulled away.

"I am sorry Jack. I shouldn't have done that." Yori apologized.

"Was my mother pretty, Yori?" Jack asked calmly. "I wonder about her sometimes."

"She was very pretty and kind of heart." Yori said smiling. "Jack, I have sad news to tell you."

"Sadness is an emotion I do not feel but please do tell me your news." Jack pleaded mostly for the conversation and company of another.

"Lilly passed away today. She was sick and had difficulties delivering her child. I know you liked her. She always treated you with kindness." Yori clenched his jaw muscles trying to stifle his emotions.

"She was very kind to me. More than she should have been." Jack said and looked down at the floor.

"Jack, there are more people locked up than my last visit. What have you heard?" Yori asked as Jack reached through the cell bars. He found the sweets Yori always brought for him. A smile crossed Jack's lips as he popped it in his mouth.

"Our brother is very angry and more dangerous than me. He will cause a rift between you and him that is irreversible. You, with your self-righteousness and he with his hypocrisy." Jack put his hand up when Yori started to interrupt. "I am getting there, be patient. The king or Henry orders Sam to imprison people for crimes they shouldn't be accused of. It is not their fault that Idris acts on feelings and impulses. Demanding taxes beyond their capabilities to pay. Enslaving their loved ones to pay the dept they owe is unjust. These actions do not bother Sam's conscious. He plays the game to stay in good favor with Idris. You will not tolerate it and can't fight it. Henceforth, you will leave the kingdom." Jack finished and walked back into the darkness and squatted in the corner. "One more thing, Yori keep the little Queen safe. The wolves will need her again."

"You know about Vada?" Yori asked surprised.

"I smelled it in her." Jack said his voice animalistic.

"I will keep her safe Jack. What can I bring you next time I visit?" Yori asked before he left.

"A live rabbit." Jack's laugh was unsettling.

"For company or lunch?" Yori asked but wasn't sure he wanted to really know the answer.

"What do you think?" Jack crept back to the cell door and brushed his hair back away from his face. "Leave the torch?" He asked and Yori placed it in the sconce behind him. "Yori." Jack stuck his face through the bars as far as he could. Yori touched Jack's nose, one of the few places he would allow contact.

"It's ok, brother I know. Until next time." Yori said pointing a finger at him. "Be good."

"Yori, don't forget to tell Jenna I said hi." He laughed ridiculously and went back to his dark corner.

"And there it is. The reminder of why your locked up. Goodbye, Jack." Yori left hearing Jack's repeated goodbyes as Yori walked away.

******

Ezra smiled when he saw Grayson and Vada riding down the path that led to Lord Andrew's farm. He clapped his hands and stepped down from the porch, happy to see his brother. Grayson dismounted and helped Vada down from her horse.

"It is so good to see you brother." Grayson said hugging Ezra. "I would like to say you look great, but you don't"

"Grayson!" Vada scolded him. "Hello, Ezra." She smiled as he kissed her cheek. "I'll see you later." She said looking back at Grayson with a scowl and went into the house to find Asia.

Come with me I want to show you something." Ezra said and Grayson followed him out to the stables. The stallion was running in circles in the arena and snorted when they approached.

"Lord Andrew gave him to me." Ezra said watching the horse dance around. "Austin and his pack ate mine."

"What?" Grayson asked shocked. "That is messed up. Sounds like we need to find Austin." Grayson said looking at the bruises that still marked his brother's face.

"I wanted the day to be perfect for her. I asked her to marry me, and we talked about building our house and about a family. I left my sword on my saddle so she would know the day was just for her. Then when Austin attacked, I didn't have it to defend us. Lord Andrew told me that he would have done the same thing I did but I still feel ashamed that she was hurt." Ezra said turning his head to look at Grayson.

Grayson turned and leaned up against the corral post. "There is going to be a lifetime of issues that will arise most of them out of your control. You can't always be where you can protect her. It would be ridiculous to believe so, Ezra. During this situation, you were being held down and beaten. The ability to protect her was taken from you whether you had your sword or not."

Ezra nodded thinking about what he had said. "You are wise brother, more so than I." He smiled and squeezed Grayson's shoulder with affection.

"No, Ezra I can just see what you can't at the moment." Grayson returned his brother's smile. They walked back toward the house stopping when a large black wolf trotted into their path. Muscles rippled beneath its coat as it transformed into a man. As he raised his head up to look at Ezra and Grayson, he brushed the hair away from his face exposing an eerie smile.

Austin whistled. "Wow! Your face looks terrible."

"Austin." Ezra acknowledged.

"Again, without your sword?" Austin stood face to face with Ezra. "Tisk, tisk, tisk." He added wagging his finger in front of his eyes. Ezra stood without emotion watching Austin with a wary eye.

"No one expected you to be this stupid, again." Grayson laughed at Austin as he moved to watch his brother's back.

"Grayson you act as though you have no trust with me." Austin retorted.

"Hard to trust a coward." Grayson flashed a smile at him over Ezra's shoulder.

"What business do you have with me, Austin?" Ezra asked interrupting their taunting.

"A chance to redeem some honor. In order to do so it must start with you." Austin motioned toward the tack room and one of his men carried out Ezra's sword and handed it to him, then handed one to Austin.

Andrew stepped out onto his porch. "And to make sure it stays fair there are archers watching you pack." He said and drew on his pipe. Austin nodded with understanding. "Grayson." Andrew waved him away from Ezra.

Grayson squared off with Austin and looked at him with a bit of madness in his eyes. "I am not as levelheaded as my brother. You cheat this time, and I will hunt you down." He turned and winked at Ezra before leaving him standing with Austin.

"Are you sure you want this?" Ezra asked smiling enjoying the feeling of his sword back in his hands.

"Let's dance." Austin said with a bow. Ezra put his hand up to pause the fight. He walked up to Austin and hit him with a solid punch to the cheek.

"That is for Asia." Ezra nodded. Austin touched his face bringing back blood on his fingertips where his cheek had split open.

"Deserved." Austin said accepting the hit knowing it was owed to him.

"You made this date. You lead." Ezra said pointing his blade at Austin. Austin was not smiling when he raised his sword to Ezra. He knew the probability of surviving this fight was null. He didn't care though. If he perished under Ezra's sword it would end the pain he carried with him that ate away at his heart. Ezra blocked the strike with ease then came at Austin with a downward thrust that caused his opponent to lose his balance and fall. Ezra stopped and stuck his hand out for Austin. "That was for my horse." Ezra said as Austin stood.

"Well, I'm glad we've got that out of the way." Austin chuckled and readied himself for the next strike. Andrew and Grayson watched as Ezra seemed to play with Austin tiring him.

"Your brother is very skilled." Andrew commented taking the pipe from his mouth. "But so are you. Yet you do not carry a blade."

Grayson kept his eyes on Ezra when he spoke to Andrew. "I will never carry a sword again. I have my reasons."

"I figure it has something to do with Joe?" Andrew prodded.

Grayson let out an audible sigh and turned his head to look at Andrew. "Joe was suffering. I had to end it." He turned his attention back toward the battle and Andrew asked no more questions. The pain in Grayson's eyes said enough. Ezra was tiring of the fight. Austin didn't have the skill level to make it a competition worthy of a lengthy battle.

"Austin, I find this no longer a fun battle and I tire of it." Ezra stuck his blade into the ground.

"Do you yield?" Austin shouted out of breath.

"Sure." Ezra said with boredom turning his back to Austin. It angered Austin to be dismissed like a child. He lunged at Ezra planning on running his blade through his back. Ezra heard Austin's feet move toward him and turned quickly around. Ezra twisted his sword around Austin's forcing him to lose grip dropping it to the ground. Ezra pointed his blade at Austin pricking the skin on his chest. Blood ran down from the wound staining his shirt. Austin looked down at his chest then back up as Ezra walked toward Austin pushing him backwards until he stumbled and fell.

Ezra was angry now. "So much for honor and trust Austin." Ezra raised his sword up to plunge it into Austin's heart.

"Ezra please!" A voice pleaded behind him.

"Give me reason!" Ezra shouted with rage; his eyes not leaving Austin.

"He's my son." It was Seth who had spoken. He walked up and placed a hand on Ezra's arm.

"He gave no thought to spare the life of Marcus or...your daughter." Ezra glared at the man under his blade. "They were my friends. You were my friend." Ezra said lowering his sword. He helped Austin to stand. "I do your father a favor by sparing your life." Ezra turned toward Seth. "I will not hesitate the next time." Andrew walked down the steps of the porch toward Seth and stopped Ezra when they met.

"You exhibited the kind of fortitude and honor that kings are made of. You're angry now Ezra, find your peace before you speak again." Andrew affectionately slapped Ezra on the back as he continued down the path to Seth. He extended his hand and Seth accepted it. "Seth you and I have known each other since time began it seems, but if that boy sets foot on my land or comes after another one of my kids including those young men there on the porch you won't be able to get to him fast enough."

"Understood, my friend." Seth nodded and shook Andrew's hand. "Our world is changing Andrew. The wolves are being pushed into the forest and will live as such until our king and queen returns. Until Vada and Grayson are ready. We will not be seen again." Seth explained with sadness.

"Grayson?" Andrew asked looking back at the porch. "He is not wolf."

"Not yet." Seth said and led his son into the woods. Andrew stood a moment looking at the brothers standing on his porch. Sara joined him with her bow still in her hand.

"What is it, Andrew?" She asked noticing the bewilderment on his face.

"It seems that we will have two sons in laws soon." Andrew looked at his wife and put his arm around her waist.

"How can that be?" She asked looking at Grayson. "He is human."

"According to Seth that will change." He smiled and kissed her cheek.

"That's not yet for us to worry about. We've to prepare for Lilly's service." Sara said when they watched Asia snuggle into Ezra's arms. "And then a wedding."

******

Idris sat with Lilly as she lay in state. He was broken-hearted and exhausted, but his tears had quite flowing. He just didn't have any more to give. Idris stood and walked up the steps to look upon her.

"Even in death you are as beautiful as the flower your name represents." A smile crossed his lips as a memory emerged. "I will always love you, Lilly. No one will ever take your place in my heart, ever." His heart died in that moment to be hers forever on the other side. He began to think about the dissension that was beginning between his favored advisors. "Something is stirring the forces of a downfall, Lilly. I can feel it. It started with our son's death and may end with mine. Your Henry, although very intelligent, doesn't have the fortitude to make the military decisions best suited for any situation, love I am sorry."

"Thank you, Father." Henry clapped. "Have you ever considered that since your love and energy poured into Marcus being your successor that I was never given a chance to receive the same dedication? I only received mondain tasks to keep me out of your way so my brother could be groomed for kingship."

"Most men were not meant to be kings, Henry." Idris said shaking his head not wanting to deal with Henry's accusations of Idris's apathy towards him.

"You seem to think highly of Ezra, often praising him for his king like nature. Why not hand your crown down to him?" Henry said throwing his hands up in the air.

"If Ezra were of my loins, he would be my next choice after Marcus. Henry, I am not having this discussion with you in this room where your mother lies in wait for her tomb." Idris walked past his son leaving him where he stood. Now angry from the encounter with Henry Idris headed to the throne room hopeful for some peace. He saw Barrett juggling another handful of cookies as he walked slowly and carefully down the hallway.

"Hello, your majesty." Barrett smiled and looked back down at the tower of cookies weaving back and forth. "Please don't tell my mother." He begged.

"I will tell you what. I will keep your secret, but it will cost you two cookies." Idris said rubbing his stomach.

"Deal." Barrett agreed. "I am sad that Queen Lilly died." The boy said looking up at the king.

"Thank you, Barrett. So am I." Idris took his cookies and then Barrett's chin in his hand. "Don't eat all those at one time it'll make your belly hurt."

"Yes, sir." Barrett said then carefully went on his way. Idris walked over to the balcony for some fresh air. Looking out over the courtyard he took in a big breath and let it out slowly. As he watched people busy with daily chores, he noticed Yori and Samuel in what seemed to be an argument. He could hear the tone but could not make out what they were saying. Their facial expressions held anger and Yori's hand were wild when he spoke. Idris snapped his fingers at a guard who was standing close by.

"Tell Lords Samuel and Yori they are to meet me in the throne room post haste." Idris watched as the guard delivered the message. They both looked up at the balcony seeing the king standing with his arms folded in front of his chest. When they walked into the throne room King Idris was sitting in his chair eating his cookies. They stood in silence before him waiting for him to speak.

"Imagine if you will how it looked from my point of view to see my two most trusted advisors publicly disputing. Now what was it all about?"

"I was merely asking Sam why so many people were being imprisoned. There is no way we have this much crime." Yori said defensively.

"Not paying taxes is a crime." Sam disputed.

"It is a crime to charge such a tax that the only way one can pay said tax is by giving up their property or being enslaved by the courts to pay off a dept owed." Yori said rubbing his forehead exhibiting stress.

"Are we back on this again? I thought this had been settled. Yori taxes had to be raised to support the seed refinery and the process of sowing the fields. Why are we reiterating all this?" Idris said shaking his head in aggravation.

"Yori believes the people will come into the city in droves overcrowding and then begin to starve." Sam said leaning up against a column.

"It has already started to happen." Yori snapped. "Prince Henry collected the deeds to twenty farms yesterday. They were also evicted, without the opportunity to collect their belongings."

"Unfortunately, that's the price they must pay to help the court with the costs of restoration of the land we inherited from the wolf nation." Idris's temper was being tested now. His knuckles whitened with the grip on his chair arms.

"You mean took, from the wolves. This all started because of the retaliation you ordered. An order that led to hundreds of lives lost. You and Samuel because of your understandable grief destroyed a nation of people." Yori said with care but knew he had taken it too far when Idris's lips tightened, and he stood up quickly.

"Are you calling the king a murderer, Yori?!" Samuel egged it with a chuckle.

"Samuel, I am calling you both murderers." Yori said through gritted teeth. "You both have caused the collapse of this kingdom!"

"Because of the very recent loss of my wife I am finding it hard to discern between what is your concern for the people or treachery of my crown. So, for the sake of our friendship and the possibility of your beheading I feel you should remove yourself from my court. You may attend Lilly's service tomorrow and then you and your family will be escorted from your residence here in this castle." Idris watched bewilderment envelope Yori's body and hurt flood his eyes. He would have never thought Idris would have denounced their friendship so easily.

"I humbly ask for your forgiveness your majesty. My mouth has obviously overrun itself. I will have my family moved by tomorrow's sunset." Yori bowed, removed the ring from his finger that signified his loyalty to the crown and tossed it to the king. Yori looked at his brother then into the eyes of his friend, seeing only coldness and anger he turned and left the room.

"My lord, I don't believe my brother would or could ever commit treason." Samuel said careful not to further anger him.

"I have had my suspicions for a while now. Yori has changed." Idris said sitting back down.

"Maybe it is we who have changed. Grief does terrible things to people." Samuel stood away from the column. "All I am asking is that you think on your decision when tempers are not so easily ignited." Samuel continued when Idris raised his eyebrow at him with warning.

******

Yori found Charles in the armory looking through the weapons collected from the raiders.

"What bee flew in your bonnet?" Charles asked as Yori slammed the door behind him and paced the floor.

"More like a couple of hornets." Yori said and explained what had transpired with Idris.

"You just got on your soapbox at the wrong time Yori. He will cool off after Lilly's service." Charles said looking up from the task at hand.

"Soapbox? What do you mean?" Yori asked with a bit of sarcasm.

"Come on Yori, sometimes you can be a little self-righteous. Not that it's a bad thing at the right time but it doesn't sound like it was." Charles shrugged.

Yori slammed his fist down on the table. "Well, I am still being evicted. Things are getting worse, Charles. You've got to see the change." Yori said picking up a sword from the loot.

"I see a season, Yori. Every life has hard times, this may be ours." He looked up at his friend weighing the blade. "But you think there's more than just hard times in our near future, don't you?"

"I am not prophesizing Charles, but I am not blind. Are you not feeling the pains of taxes? Do you not see the people begging for food in the streets?" Yori looked side-eyed at Charles.

"Aye, it does not go unnoticed." Charles sighed.

"So, you chose to ignore it as you belly up to the kings table?" Yori challenged his friend. Charles straightened his back and looked cross at his friend.

"Now Yori, before you step on any more toes today maybe you should go elsewhere and cool your temper." Charles advised taking the sword from Yori and laying it back down on the table.

"I saw Jack. He said that people are flooding into the dungeons by Sams hand, his orders coming from Henry or Idris or both. Not sure which one but it doesn't matter. I refuse to keep my family in a kingdom that has beliefs that its people are worthless and disposable for the sake of financial gain." Yori said as he opened the door to leave. "I am riding out to Andrew's to get my sons then to my farm to prepare it for our move." He started out the door then stopped. "Charles, I am not trying to create problems where none lay. Your eyes will open soon enough." Charles rubbed the stubble on is chin, walked over to the door and sighed. Yori was an insightful man. He knew there was truth in what Yori believed but wasn't sure it was to the extreme he cautioned. Charles went to the sables and saddled his horse. He would ride and try to see what Yori saw. As he rode out of the courtyard Charles noticed the stress and heavy loads that the citizens seem to bear. Children were crying, reaching for food as he went by. Wives of men that rode with the king's army stood watching him pass with worried expressions. Most of the shops that normally were busy with business were closed and boarded up. This was happening fast. The toll of the wolf kingdom's demise was weighing on the people and Idris seemed to be absorbing the suffering like it was nourishment. Yori was right. Charles encouraged his horse to gallop catching up with him. Arriving at Andrews farm just minutes behind Yori he saw several families that were there and more could be seen down the road. Yori watched Charles ride up and walked over to him.

"I have seen what you have Yori. I am sorry I did not listen with an open mind. Obviously, I have not felt the pinch of taxes yet to understand the circumstances of others." Charles said, dismounting.

"I am glad you are here Charles. Let's see what issue has bombarded our friend." Yori said slapping Charles on the back with affection. A commotion of loud voices came from the front porch of Andrews home.

"Father, Lord Charles." Ezra greeted them.

"Catch me up." Yori said and waited for Ezra to finish speaking before walking up to the group. Grayson nodded at his father and Charles acknowledging them.

"Yori, how are we supposed to feed our families? Our land was the only source of food we had. We had a garden so bountiful we could have shared it with others. Prince Henry brought out troops and gathered it all. Not even a bean left on the vine. Then he evicted us by taking our home for past due taxes. How could we have past due taxes if it hasn't even been a month. How can the king allow such atrocity?" He was so distraught tears were welling up in his eyes. Other farmers chimed in on their current conditions.

"Some can stay here. I have room in the barn and those who have sheltered wagons can find a place to hold up until we can figure this out." Andrew announced.

"Aye, I offer mine as well." Charles said, raising his hand.

"I do not know the status of my land yet. I have not been there in some time but am willing to do the same." Yori offered.

"Do not offer up a plan of any kind to depart the kingdom if that is in your thoughts. Be still with it for a bit longer." Charles advised quietly for Yori's ears only. "You know not who is trustworthy."

"It has only been a short time since the king imposed the outrages tax upon us. If the court decides to continue such demand, we shall all parish." Another spoke with a worrisome tone. "What can we do?" They all looked at Yori.

"For now, you all will stay with us. We will make sure you have the food you need for your families. Give us time to come up with a plan." Yori said and looked at his sons. He saw no other way but to leave. He had lost his position with Idris and his friendship. What was lost is lost for good. His family would have to start new elsewhere. "Ezra, Grayson." He motioned for them to follow him. "Andrew, I shall return in two days. Charles will explain."

Ezra and Grayson followed their father to the horses. "I brought you a horse to ride for now Ezra."

After riding a distance Ezra finally asked. "Why do you no longer wear your ring, Father?"

"I accused the king of murder. He wasn't pleased so he has discharged me. With further quarrel he banished my family from the castle. That is why we travel to the farm, to prepare it for your mother to make it a home once more. Or at least until I figure something else out." Yori said stopping his horse.

"So, all of us have lost our jobs?" Ezra asked looking at his father in disbelief.

"I am afraid so, Ezra. Yori answered and watched as Ezra dropped his head. He opened his mouth to speak but decided not to and rode away. Yori looked at Grayson.

"You always seem to have good reasons for what you do father, this issue however will affect many." Grayson gestured toward his brother. "Your eldest was in line to be an advisor to Marcus upon his succession as king, to be married to Asia, have a family, and a farm of his own. Even though you had nothing to do with Marcus's fate, you have altered the rest. So, what are your plans to fix this?"

"Leave the kingdom. Start over by the sea." Yori said as he started his horse walking again.

"Leave?" Grayson asked surprised, snapping his head around to look at his father. "And you expect Ezra and I to follow?"

"Yes, you both are my sons." Yori said expecting no quarrel.

"Grown sons, with plans of our own. I sir, will not leave without my brother...or Vada." Grayson said sternly and urged his horse to catch up with Ezra.

"Well, I have to admit my surprise by that turn of events." Yori mumbled to himself as he rode a steady pace behind them. Yori looked ahead to see Ezra and Grayson stopped on the top of the hill overlooking his farmhouse. Cautiously, he rode up next to them and saw what had stopped them. Several men were busy below loading wagons with weapons. They had been stashed away in Yori's barn and were to travel back to the castle. Yori saw it was best to wait until they had left before taking his sons into the nest of thieves. "Let's wait down by the river for them to leave." Yori said quietly. He watched his sons turn to leave then glanced back at the house. Samuel had come out onto the porch stretching. He shouted at someone in anger and then proceeded to his horse. After mounting the animal, he looked around. His head stopped when he saw Yori on the hillside. They both sat still looking at one another knowing from that moment forth their relationship as brothers was over. Yori turned his horse away and followed his sons. Grayson picked up a suitable stick and began sharpening the end to a point. Not speaking he walked down to the river. Ezra gathered bark and stones to build a fire. The night was urgently stealing the day giving way to the stars. Crickets and frogs sang their nightly melody as the three men ate the fish that Grayson had speared. When Grayson finished, he picked up his bow and slipped into the darkness.

Ezra stood. "Tis your plan to stay the night here?" He asked his father.

"Tis." Yori answered and stopped his son when Ezra walked away. "Ezra, you have every right to be angry."

"You misinterpret my silence, Father. The decision you made to insult the king has inadvertently changed the course of my life. I am now unable to support a wife and will have to put off a wedding. I am sure you understand the wrath I will be faced with. So, Father it is not anger you sense but fear." Ezra said with a slight smile crossing his lips. He turned away then looked over his shoulder at Yori. "There is one more thing Father, that I must make perfectly clear. I am my own man; you may not make decisions for my life anymore. Understood?"

Yori stood and looked Ezra in the eye. "You are understood." He took the reins of his horse and walked into the darkness of the woods. Ezra looked at the stars and sighed. He knew he had hurt his father, but it was time to set those boundaries.

******

Yori eased up slowly to where Grayson stood leaning against a tree.

"There hasn't been any movement in a while. I believe all to be gone." Grayson whispered.

"Tell Ezra we shall stay the night in the house instead. I'll head down to secure the house." Yori said and patted Grayson's back. As he watched his son walk back down the hill, he began to think about the conversation he had with Ezra. He really didn't know how to feel about it. His son was right though. Both sons were old enough to make their own decisions and whatever they decided to do about leaving the kingdom he would have to accept. Yori smiled, he had to admit he was proud of Ezra for standing up for himself. There was a poster tacked to the door when he arrived at the house. He pulled it off and went inside. Lighting the lantern, he sat down and read it. It was a seize order on his land for nonpayment of taxes signed by his majesty the king and dated with today's date. "You wasted no time consummating the disillusion of our friendship Idris." He looked up at Ezra and Grayson when they walked inside the house. "You both have a decision to make." He handed the poster to them. "I have no other choice now. I will be leaving in the morning to get your mother and Barrett from the castle. In a few days' time I will be heading to the coast. Whoever wishes to start a new life may join us." Yori stood stretching out his back. "That being said I am going to sleep."

"Goodnight Father." Ezra said laying the paper down on the table.

"He's had it handed to him of late." Grayson said sitting and pulling off his boots.

"Yes, and I didn't help any today." Ezra said feeling badly about confronting his father. He had the upmost respect for him and just needed Yori to see him as a man.

"How so?" Grayson asked looking up at his brother.

"I asked him not to make decisions for me anymore." Ezra said, taking his sword from his back and hanging it by the door.

"That's a reasonable request." Grayson shrugged lying on the floor and crossing his ankles.

"Well, yes, but it seems a little cruel considering all he's been through." Ezra said rubbing his neck.

"Ez look, I don't think he has realized yet that we are adults. Thanks to him we're able to make our own life choices. It will just take some adjustments is all." Grayson said peeking out from under his arm that lay over his face. Ezra blew out the lantern and walked outside. The bugs still sang their lullabies under the full moon. At times it was so loud he wanted to shout at them to quiet their songs. A panther screamed a bone chilling cry into the night raising the hair on the back of his neck. It seemed as close as the river below. Ezra lay in the grass and looked up at the stars and began to think. Marcus's death had set forth a chain of events that had altered all their lives not just his. His father, who fought for the people and stood up against wrong was relieved of his duties not only as an advisor of the king but a lifetime friendship with Idris. He didn't see his father as running, just stepping back out of the way. Maybe, the kingdom needs to fall to realize how good it had been. His father wanted to take the good people away from the destruction he saw coming. It was all becoming clear to Ezra, his father's vision. He sighed feeling like a cad. He will talk to Asia tomorrow. Ezra knew now he would follow his father. He just hoped she would go with him.

******

Grayson was awakened in the night by a familiar voice. When he opened his eyes, Seth was standing over him. "Come." He extended his hand down to Grayson and helped him stand. Grayson picked up his bow and quiver as they left the house. They passed Ezra asleep in the grass. "Do you boys have a problem with beds?" Seth asked quietly. Grayson followed him into the depths of the woods. When he stopped his wife, Amanda came from behind a large tree. A smaller woman followed her. She wore a white linen gown with a hood edged in black fur that draped over the top of her head. Her hair, long and black, was embellished with baby's breath. It hung in a braid down the front of her bodice to her waist. She looked up at him through those big, beautiful eyes of hers and bit the side of her lip. Seth had to call his name a couple of times before Grayson heard him.

"What is this all about?" Grayson asked, his eyes still connected to Vada's.

"I am sorry this must be rushed and without your families present or further explanation, we are running out of time." Amanda said positioning Grayson beside Vada.

"Whoa! Someone is going to make time right now." Grayson said stepping back.

"Has it not called to your heart to wed Vada?" Seth asked.

"It has but we have not known each other long." Grayson said looking at Vada and the fear in her eyes.

"Grayson, Vada, I understand you are young and your feelings for each other new. believe me when I say that your love has been foretold." Seth said with conviction.

"Vada your mother asked us to perform the ceremony. She asks that you trust in us." Amanda said, taking her hand. "All answers you seek will be revealed as your lives unfold." She placed Vada's hand in Grayson's and loosely bound their hands together. She then draped an embroidered cloth with royal symbols across the top of their joined hands.

Grayson looked into Vada's eyes. "I guess were getting married."

"Looks that way indeed." She smiled back at him. "My heart is good with it."

"As is mine." Grayson said touching the side of her face with his other hand. Seth began to chant, neither one of them understanding what it was he said, but trusted it was good. When he stopped, they both looked at him for the next steps, he chuckled.

Amanda removed the wedding cloth and freed their hands. "Kiss your bride, Grayson." she instructed.

"That I understand." Grayson said as he quickly drew her in to him kissing her passionately.

"We know that your father intends to leave for the coast. You must go with him; your destiny awaits you there. Take this path." Seth pointed. "We have readied you a private place for the rest of the night." Seth put his hand at the small of his wife's back and led her into the darkness.

"Do you find this strange?" Vada asked Grayson as they started down the directed path.

"People are always that way around me, it's like they all know this life altering secret, but won't reveal what it is." Vada smiled and shrugged one shoulder.

"It is strange that our marriage has been rushed. But Vada I feel we would have eventually reached this day. I do love you." He said, taking her hand.

"I love you too." She smiled shyly. They found a makeshift bed made of leaves and flower petals not far from where they were wed. Captured fireflies danced in the lanterns hanging from tree limbs. Beautiful cloth lay across the bushes around the bed giving an extra bit of privacy.

"We don't have to do anything if you are not ready." Grayson said sensing her hesitance.

"I have already shared a bed with you, it is not that. Tonight, just happened so quickly my mind is still trying to sort it all out." Vada looked up at him and saw the warmth in his eyes.

"We could just share the night if you like. They made us a beautiful spot. It would be a shame not to use it." Grayson said, leading her to the bed. They laid down facing each other and she blushed at the way he looked at her. It was as if she was a sweet treat, and he was hungry.

"When will you stop blushing when I look at you with desire?" He asked, touching her lips with his gently.

"I do not know. Maybe, when we've been married a thousand years." She touched the side of his face gently with her hand and then tugged on his beard. "When will you stop looking at me the way you are now?"

"When I breath no more and my bones are bleached by the sun, then maybe." Grayson smiled, tucking her hair behind her ear. He rubbed his finger over the ambulant.

"It was my mothers'." Vada said looking at it with him. "Where did you get that scar?" Vada asked tracing it in his eyebrow.

Grayson chuckled at the memory. "Ezra, he shot me with an arrow when we were kids." Grayson touched her chin sliding his fingers down her neck to the tie on her bodice. Slowly, he pulled it undone. When she allowed him to push the material from her shoulders he kissed them gently. He slipped his shirt off and threw it to the side. Vada felt his chest and the tight muscles of his stomach, and she felt an ache for him. When her fingers stopped just below his waistline Grayson groaned.

"I don't know what my future self has done to deserve you Vada, but I will have to remember to thank him one day." Grayson whispered as he freed her breasts from their bondage then rolled her on top of him. He wanted to feel her against his chest skin on skin.

Vada propped her head up on his chest with her arm. "I feel this thing you and I have started here will last a lifetime." Vada smiled and ran her fingertip over his lips.

"Aye, my sweet." Grayson agreed and noticed the moonlight filtering through the leaves above giving her hair a magical aura of sorts. "What powers do you have that have me so mesmerized by your beauty." Vada ran her fingers through his hair and kissed him lovingly. Grayson pulled the soft material of her skirt up to her waist feeling the softness of her lower back and bottom. She untied her hair from its braid and let it cascade over her back. Grayson felt his passion rise as she reached between their hips and took him in her hands. "Is this your consent, my lady?" He asked as she caressed him.

"Tis, my husband." She answered and he raised her hips to lower her down on him. She looked into his eyes with longing as she received him. A wolf's howl echoed throughout the night creating a surge of wild passion igniting her blood. She felt as though she was on fire and threw her head back as Grayson rose up to meet her. She felt a fury inside that cried to be set free and she met every thrust Grayson brought forth. Vada looked over Grayson's shoulder to see a black wolf in the shadows. Its eyes seemed to be glowing. She felt a connection to the animal, familiarity. Vada watched the wolf as if in a trance until Grayson turned her onto her back. The wolf walked around them, and Grayson cried out as he felt a stinging sensation of markings engraving his shoulders and down his arms. As it continued to circle them Grayson saw its movement and watched it move slowly. Their eyes locked and he felt a draw to the nature of the wolf, the primal need to connect with the wild surged within him. This feeling of untamed essence flowed through him and into Vada as they reached their release together.

******

Ezra heard a wagon approaching as the sun adorned the treetops with a glorious hue. He recognized his little brother's voice as they came up the road and decided to pretend he was still sleeping.

"Look Mother, Ezra still sleeps." Barrett laughed jumping down from the wagon.

"You should wake him. No one should be still abed when the sun arises. Am I right?" Clara said with humor.

"Yes Mother." He giggled and snuck up quietly to Ezra and jumped on his belly.

"Mother help! Help! I have been attacked!" Ezra shouted as he grabbed Barrett tickling him. "I have missed you little brother."

"Ezra, I brought breakfast, meant for Idris's table. It is in the wagon. Please take it into the house." She said gathering her skirts as he assisted her from the wagon.

"Yes, Mother." Ezra winked and smiled at her. "Mother did you steal this meal?"

"I am sure I don't know what you are talking about, son." She said raising her nose up.

"I'm sure." Ezra nodded.

Clara saw her husband on the porch steps and went to him.

"I was getting ready to ride in for you and Barrett." Yori said kissing her cheek.

"We were awakened by guards in the wee hours of the morning demanding that we vacate the castle immediately. Yori I barely had time to fasten my buttons. They wouldn't let me take any of our belongings or any of your writings that were in the desk were seized by the guards. After all the years of service and friendship and this is the way we were treated. If Lilly were here this would have never happened." Clara said in a huff. "And Sam said to tell you cannot return not even to see Jack. They will be watching him. I think they are afraid you would free your brother."

"That is ridiculous! Jack should never be freed unless by death." Yori scoffed. "I am sorry my love that you were treated harshly." He took her face in his hands and kissed her lips. "How did you know I was here?"

"Sam. He said you and the boys were here. He also said that we couldn't stay. There would be men here early afternoon to force us out. Yori why can't we stay?" She asked with concern fighting back the tears that threatened to fall.

Yori took her hands and kissed the tops of them. "The king has placed a seize order on our farm for taxes."

"I know you have a plan my love." She said smiling. "You always do."

"Leave. Head to the coast and start a new life. I can't fight this, Clara. All I can do is lead whoever wants to follow. Maybe, someday we can come back but for now we must leave." Yori pulled her up against him smiling and slightly tipped his head sideways. "Think of it as a long awaited vacation." He pushed his hips against her and she felt him swollen and wanting.

"Our children are close by, Yori." Clara whispered, smacking his chest.

"Hasn't stopped us before." Yori cupped her face in his hand and drew her in for a sensuous kiss.

"Ewwww, gross." Barrett said of his parents kissing.

"One day that will be you, Barrett. Kissing a girl...on the lips!" Ezra teased his little brother.

"No way! I will never kiss a girl, yuck!" Barrett said shaking his head in disgust.

"Come on little brother let's eat." Ezra told him as he opened the door, taking the basket of food with him. Yori put his arm around Clara's waist, and they walked in behind their sons.

"Where is Grayson?" Clara asked as she placed dishes around the table.

"He left in the middle of night with Lord Seth." Ezra replied, helping Barrett with his food.

"Seth?" Clara said with surprise and quickly looked at Yori, which didn't go unnoticed by Ezra.

"What?" Ezra asked looking at each of them.

"Seth must have sensed we were leaving. That's the only reason…" Clara said, filling Yori's cup with coffee.

"Do I need to find my brother?" Ezra asked, not liking the look on his mother's face.

"No, Ezra. He is fine. Just probably married." Yori said sitting down beside Barrett ruffling his hair.

"Married?" Ezra said choking on his food.

"Are you ok, Ezra?" Barrett asked patting his brother on the back.

"I am good thank you bubba." Ezra said and cleared his throat. "What do you mean married?"

"Vada's mother made Seth and Amanda promise that Seth would be the one to marry Vada to the man Salora had chosen." Clara said being careful not to say too much.

"Which I am assuming is Grayson. Wait..I thought Vada's mother had died." Ezra said, trying to remember the story.

"She did." Yori said and looked cautiously at his wife.

"Ohhhhh she's a ghost!" Barrett shouted, putting his hands to either side of his face and wiggled his fingers.

"She's a mystical creature of sorts neither alive nor dead. If you believe in such things." Yori said sipping his coffee.

"And you're ok with your son being married to her daughter?" Ezra asked surprised in how dismissive they were. There was more than they were saying, he believed.

"I like Vada. She's nice." Barrett said frowning at Ezra. "Can I have Grayson's biscuit?" He asked rubbing his hands together. "Ha! Ha! Grayson, it's mine." Barrett laughed sinking his teeth into the bread.

"It's obvious you both know more than you are willing to tell so as long as my brother is in no harm I will let it be." Ezra said with defeat.

******

Grayson felt a tickle across his mustache waking him from sleep. A quiet giggle reminded him of the night before and a smile crossed his lips.

"Good morning wife." He said opening his eyes to her beautiful face.

"Good morning husband." She returned the greeting. She popped a strawberry in his mouth.

"Where did you find strawberries?" He asked propping himself up on an elbow.

She shrugged. "They were here when I awoke. Strawberries, grapes, blueberries." Grayson took the basket of fruit and sat it to the side. He gently touched the side of her face tracing her lips as she ate the berry. She had not fixed her bodice leaving her breast still exposed to him. Vada crawled upon his lap and pressed her body against his. He stood with her and she wrapped her legs around his waist. Her gown flowed down past her bottom and brushed the ground as he carried her down to the river.

"Grayson, fill me with your desire." She begged, her warm breath on his neck encouraging him to oblige her. She caught her breath when he lowered her into the cool water. She reached below the water and took him in her hand and a smile crossed his lips when he felt her rub him gently.

"Your touch is like silk my lady. If you're not careful you will not get the fill you requested." Grayson warned taking her breasts in his hands. He circled the tips with his fingers and then devoured them with his mouth. She cried out and he moved her up on the shore unable to wait any longer to be inside of her. Afterwards, they lay on the shore warming in the morning sun kissing and holding each other. Grayson stopped when he heard his horse whinny. He searched through the trees looking for it. Then he saw Ezra riding leading Grayson's horse behind him. "It's Ezra. He is looking for us." Grayson said standing. He held his hand down to help her stand. Grayson whistled, getting his brother's attention.

"Mother sent me for you." Ezra said, handing his brother the reins to his horse. "Vada." Ezra said nodding but did not smile. "You are to meet our family at lord Andrew's property.'" Ezra turned his horse to leave then stopped but didn't turn around. "I suppose congratulations are in order." He said though his tone did not convey his sentiment.

"Ezra." Grayson said stepping toward him, but Ezra rode away leaving him standing there.

"I think we have hurt him with our marriage." Vada said as Grayson tossed her up on the horse.

"How so?" He asked climbing up behind her.

"He's done everything the right way. The ring, the proposal, planning their lives together and we come in and kind of steal his thunder." Vada said pulling his arm up around her waist.

"I see. Maybe we should just keep it to ourselves a while then." Grayson shrugged. "Are you ok with that?"

"Yes, but I will tell Asia and her parents. I will not sleep without my husband at my side." She said and reached for her ambulant. "Grayson! My ambulant..it's gone!" She searched her clothing and didn't find it.

"Let's go back to where we slept. I am sure it is there." Grayson turned his horse around and they watched the ground to see if she had dropped it as they went to the river.

"There! Grayson, I see it." Vada hopped down and grabbed it quickly as if it was sinking into the ground. Grayson pulled her back up with him.

She was quiet and kept looking down at the ambulant. "It is broken." She said sadly.

"I am sorry Vada." Grayson said and kissed her cheek.

"It's the only thing I have that belonged to my mother." She pulled it to her chest and leaned up against him as they rode out of the woods.

******

"It has begun. That ambulant wasn't broken, it is opening." Seth said watching them ride away. Salora appeared beside them and smiled. "Your daughter will turn soon. I worry about her with no instructions on how to handle the change."

"They will reach their destination before she does." Salora smiled confidently and turned to walk away.

"I wish we could be here to see it unfold." Amanda said taking Seth's hand and following Salora.

"Come my family." Salora simply said and transformed into wolf. Seth kissed his wife then together transformed as well. They disappeared into the forest and faded to the other side.

******

"Ezra," Grayson called after his brother as he headed to the tack room. "Ezra! Face me." Grayson was irritated and raised his voice. Ezra stopped and slowly turned to look at his brother. "Tell me why you are angry with me."

"I am not angry with you, Grayson." Ezra slapped his leg with his riding gloves.

"Really? Because you seem to be. I've never seen you rude to anyone before today. You owe Vada an apology." Grayson said with a calmer tone and pointing at his brother. Yori had seen them walk inside together and waited outside the building and listened.

"You are right, she did nothing to deserve my sour mood. I will apologize to her. And I am not angry with you Gray. I'm not even angry. Disappointment is a word better suited." Ezra sat down on a barrel and looked at his hands. "I have decided to follow father to the new lands. In doing so I cannot give Asia the wedding I had planned. I'm not even sure she will want to go. I haven't been able to steal her away even for a moment to find out."

"Ez, do you really think Asia cares how grand her wedding is? I believe she would marry you this very second if you asked her." Grayson said as Asia walked up next to him.

"She would and follow you to the ends of the earth Ezra, son of Yori." Asia said with a smile as Ezra looked up when hearing her voice. Grayson nodded at his brother then left them to talk.

Yori caught him as he left the tack room. "I've not had time to talk with you, son. Congratulations on your marriage to Vada."

"Thank you, Father. It was very surprising to say the least. I don't understand the urgency to wed before we left but Seth spoke of a prophecy that we would be together forever. It felt right in my heart, and I do love her." Grayson explained as they watched Charles and Marcy pull up in their wagon. Charles was grumbling when he stepped down and helped his wife off the wagon.

"We've been unlawfully evicted! By that little weasel they like to call a Prince. Marcy and I gathered all the food we could before they forced us to go. We will be following you when you leave Yori." Charles said shaking his friend's hand.

"Oh, I wanted to turn that young man over my knee, I did." Marcy said angrily as she adjusted her skirts and marched to the house.

Andrew bowed slightly to her as they passed one another. "My lady."

"My lord." She acknowledged still angry, her skirts swooshing loudly as she walked.

"Yori almost half of the kingdom is here or on their way. Word has traveled like wildfire of your departure to new lands." Andrew said, joining his companions.

"How has this happened so quickly? To be lords of lands and leaders in the courts one day and penniless and homeless the next." Charles shook his head in disbelief.

"I think something has been going on for some time, then when Prince Marcus was killed it just opened the door to the evil side of it." Andrew shrugged, drawing on his pipe.

"Aye, Andrew, I believe you are probably right about that and if word is spreading this fast, it goes to reason that Idris has already heard. I suggest my friends that we should leave first thing in the morning." Yori suggested.

******

"My ladies," Vada curtsied approaching Clara and Sara. "If it is true about our departure tomorrow morn, I implore you to give Ezra and Asia a wedding today." Clara looked at Sara and smiled slyly.

"This we can do!" Sara stood with excitement. "Listen up ladies." She said gathering them all around. "We've got a wedding to put together!"

"I will find Asia." Vada giggled and went outside to look for her. She saw her coming out of the tack room with Ezra holding her hand. She was laughing at something he said and then stopped to kiss him. "Asia? I have news." Vada said clapping her hands.

"What is it?" Asia asked, curious of her excitement.

"The ladies are preparing a wedding for you and Ezra, today!" Vada took Asia's hand. "Come on sister we must ready you to walk down the aisle." Asia blew Ezra a kiss as Vada pulled her away from him.

******

Ezra stood nervously awaiting his bride to walk down the aisle. He wore a long flowing white shirt that buttoned all the way up to the standing collar, which was embellished with black and silver threads. Ezra's head was shaved from the tops of the ears down and the top of his hair was braided down the back of his neck. His mustache circled around his mouth into a goatee with silver and black beads braided into it. These were the colors he had chosen for his family. Ezra glanced over at his father and brothers who stood at his side. He smiled at them and rocked back and forth on his heels waiting for Asia. He made eye contact with his mother and winked at her. Music began to play, and Ezra felt his knees buckle. He had been dreaming of this moment since he had met her. Vada and Jenna walked up and stood at Asia's side. When Vada's eyes made contact with Grayson's, she blushed. Then Ezra saw Asia. His beautiful bride. He was mesmerized by her beauty and could not take his eyes from hers. The dress she wore was sleeveless with little loops of white material that fell from her shoulders. The neckline on the bodice was low cut and it raised her breasts. Her skirt was slim and fit Asia's body perfectly. A cape fastened to the back of her dress complimented her tiny frame. Her long hair flowed freely, adorned with a beautiful veil that was attached to a tiara. Her father had her arm but now Ezra had her heart.

"Ezra, son of Yori, I entrust my daughter's hand to you now. Honor me by protecting her always and loving her forever." Andrew said and kissed his daughter on the cheek. He placed her hand in Ezra's and lightly tied a binding rope around their hands. Sara laid a long narrow cloth embroidered with wedding symbols across the rope. Charles spoke over the couple and Ezra didn't hear a word he said. He stared into her eyes and was lost in them, so much so that he didn't hear Charles when his name was called. "Ezra." Charles touched his arm. When Ezra looked at him Charles continued. "You are now husband and wife. You may kiss your bride." Applause broke out when Ezra pulled her in quickly to him and kissed her. Charles removed the cloth and draped it over Ezra's shoulders. After the rope was removed Ezra took Asia's hand and kissed her again.

"I love you so very much, Asia." Ezra grinned.

"I love you too." She laid her forehead against his and laughed. "We finally did it." She said excitedly.

"You look stunning." Ezra said as his eyes wandered to her breasts.

"Ezra love, my eyes are up here." Asia pointed at her face and giggled.

"Your eyes are indeed beautiful, but so are they." Ezra said in a whisper. "I can't wait to have you all to myself." He put his hand on the small of her back and they greeted the people.

Yori shook his son's hand and spoke quietly that he would be leaving in the night to see Jack. "Grayson is following to watch my back."

"Father, I will go as well." Ezra said keeping their conversation quiet.

"No, Ezra this is your wedding night. I just wanted you to know so if I don't come back, I expect you to lead these people to the new lands." Yori said patting his son on the back.

Ezra nodded. "Just make sure you come back."

******

"I wasn't sure you would come." Jack said with excitement but then realized it was his last visit with his brother. "You are here to say goodbye aren't you Yori?" Jack's tone changed to sadness.

"I am." Yori glanced around to make sure they were alone. "I am sorry, I cannot stay long. Sam has eyes upon you, luckily, some are still loyal to me. I have never known Idris to be so cruel so quickly. How have I been so blind to his many personalities?"

"When people fall into the madness realm of grief, sometimes they don't return. Idris was a gentle king until he lost the ones, he loved the most." Jack put his head against the bars and sniffed. "That includes you, Yori." Jack reached through the bars and took the cloth sack from his hand.

"Clara packed all that for you. I think there is a pie in there too." Yori smiled at Jack's excitement.

"Tell her thank you." It was hard for Jack to say but he liked his brother's wife.

"I have something else for you Jack." Yori said and pulled a vial out of his pocket.

"Is that death?" Jack asked looking out of the corner of his eyes.

"For a mortal man, yes. Jack, I don't know what effect it will have on you. It's a chance you must decide its worth." Yori handed him the vial through the bars. After Jack snatched the poison from his brother, he took Yori's hand and placed it on top of his head.

Yori smiled as he rubbed Jack's head. "I love you, Jack."

"Father, we must go." Grayson said with urgency as he approached Yori. Jack jumped at the cage to see who had spoken. He sniffed inhaling deeply.

"This boy is yours, Yori?" Jack asked, his eyes wild.

"This is Grayson." Yori introduced.

"Uncle Jack." Grayson bowed.

"I smell wolf on you boy." Jack growled, then smiled at his nephew. "Was she good?"

"Jack that's enough." Yori cautioned. Jack reached through the cell motioning Grayson to come closer. When Grayson was within his grasp Jack grabbed him by his shirt and slammed him against the cell. His eyes warned Yori away as he whispered into Grayson's ear. Jack slapped Grayson gently on the side of his face and pushed him away laughing.

"Goodbye brother, maybe on the other side my mind will be better." Jack said rolling his head around and rubbing his neck. Yori saw the bite marks the rats had left on his brother's arms and his heart was saddened.

"Goodbye, Jack." Yori smiled one last time at his youngest brother.

"Leave the torch." Jack demanded as they walked away. Grayson placed the torch in the sconce. He looked back at his uncle thinking about what he had told him.

"Goodbye, Grayson." Jack said slipping back into the darkness of the cell.

"Goodbye, Uncle." Grayson said as he followed Yori down the darkened hall. Jack took a piece of bread from the sack and looked over the vial.

"Hello." Jack turned the vial of poison around in his fingers. After studying it a moment he uncorked it and smelled the orderless contents. "What shall I do with you, my friend. Would you show me kindness and allow me an eternal slumber? Or, are you a trickster happy to twist my thoughts more than they presently are. I wonder your indications and if I shouldn't test them first." He poured a couple droplets onto the bread and tossed it across the room. "Eat upon the bread tonight instead of me my friends." Jack stretched out his legs on the floor and pulled the pie from the sack. He watched as the rodents devoured the bread. He clapped as they began wobbling around the cell as if drunk off wine. His humor faded though when the rats began to claw at their eyes with pain blinding themselves. Blood ran from their sockets and was smelled by a mischief of rats. Jack watched as they ate their wounded companions.

"Jack, pour out the vial." A sweet voice whispered to him. "How can you come to me if your body rots in the ground?" A beautiful woman sat down beside him. She took the vial and emptied the contents onto the cell floor. Jack laid his head in her lap and she played with his hair.

"You are right, Jenna. You are always right." He smiled while eating his pie.

"Who are you talking to in there?" A guard asked, banging on the cell door.

"Tell me misguided loyal servant to the king. Do you see anyone else but me?" Jack asked, hiding his pie.

"No, I do not." He answered, holding his torch in the cell to see into the corners.

"Then it doesn't matter with whom I am converting with. Go about your business." Jack shooed him away. "Now where were we?"

The guard heard Jack continue his conversation with his imaginary friend as he walked down the hall. "Crazy as a loon that one."

******

"Yori!" Samuel shouted at him as his brother started to mount his horse. Yori stepped back down to the ground and only had to look at Grayson for him to slip into the shadows.

"Sam, a little past your bedtime, isn't it?" Yori asked, taking off his gloves and tucking them in his belt.

"I could say the same of you. I gave your wife a message that you were to stay clear of Jack." Samuel said resting his hand on the hilt of his sword.

"I'm leaving Sam. You and Idris have made it perfectly clear that I have been ostracized. I only wanted to let Jack know I wouldn't be back. I wish you would come with me Samuel." Yori took a step forward and Samuel put his hand up to stop him.

"You made your choices, Yori. I am devoted to the king unlike you. I will not be the traitor you have turned out to be." Samuel said sadly. "You shame me brother."

"Sam let me ask you who the traitor really is in this little scenario, me for standing up for the people, Idris for betraying said people or you, brother, for choosing a tyrant king over family?" Yori asked with distaste.

Sam drew his sword and pointed it at Yori. "Are you challenging me brother?" Sam shouted in anger. He stepped forward and placed the tip of his blade on Yori's chest.

"No." Yori simply said and walked away. He placed his foot in the stirrup, gave Samuel a pained expression as he threw his leg over the saddle and rode away.

"Coward!" Samuel yelled after him.

"Sam," Charles said riding out of the darkness behind him. "You and I both know if he had chosen to fight you, you would be dead right now." He urged his horse into a trot and followed Yori.

******

"You should be with your bride, Ezra." Andrew said, stopping his horse where Ezra watched for his father's return.

"I cannot give her the attention she deserves while I worry about his safety. He rode to see Jack." Ezra said, turning his head to look at Andrew.

"Yes, I know. I also know that Grayson and Charles rode with him. He will return, Ezra." Andrew said knocking the old tobacco out of his pipe.

"What made you decide to follow my father to the new lands?" Ezra wondered.

He chuckled as he lit a newly packed pipe. "Well," He paused to draw on it. "For one, his sons are taking two of my daughters. For another, Yori is one of my dearest friends. If he believes it is best for us to leave, then it is so." Andrew said and pointed over his star lit land. "This all became mine when I was about your age, Ezra. But land is only borrowed for a time. This is mine now but soon someone else will come along and make it theirs, work it, change it." He shrugged. "It is the way of the world. As a young man that may be hard to think that way, but you will someday."

"I appreciate your wisdom, my lord. It has been a struggle seeing past my own disappointments of late. I made promises to you that I cannot keep. My plans to provide for Asia have been altered in the blink of an eye. Who I was becoming changed and left me with nothing to give her." Ezra looked back into the darkness avoiding eye contact.

"Son, you are grieving over a life that would have led you down a path of destruction. Be thankful that your father closed that door for you." Andrew stopped and looked at his son-in-law. "Ezra, you bring no shame upon me. I know you will protect and provide for my daughter." Then Andrew chuckled and Ezra turned and looked at him puzzled. "But it may be you that needs protection if you do not get back to your bride on her wedding night. I will watch for Yori."

Ezra smiled and slightly bowed. He turned his horse to leave. "Yes, my lord you are right." Ezra urged his horse forward and trotted back to the house. Vada was sitting on the porch swing when he rode up to the house. Dismounting, he handed the reins over to another that took his horse to the corral. Ezra looked at her with shame as he walked up the steps. He took off his gloves and stuck them in the side of his boot.

"Sister, it has been brought to my attention that I was very rude earlier. I assure you, my lady, it was not my intentions. I am sorry." Ezra bowed.

Vada smiled at him. "Ezra, I understand your distress and didn't think anything of it. But thank you sir for your kindness." Vada smiled warmly. "My sister awaits you in her room." Vada winked.

"What of you? Did we kick you out of your bed?" Ezra asked, looking back at her after opening the door.

"No, Grayson and I are kicking Jenna from hers." She laughed. "I'm just enjoying the night waiting on my husband."

"Goodnight then." Ezra nodded and went inside. Asia was sitting in front of her mirror brushing her hair when he entered the bedroom. The stiffness in her back told him she was not pleased with his tardiness. He took the brush from her hand and began to brush gently. "Forgive me, Asia. I was holding council with your father and watching for the return of mine. I realize it is our wedding night, I am truly sorry." He sighed and kissed the top of her head. She stood and put her arms around his neck.

"I am not mad really Ezra. But I do intend that you make it up to me." She said, biting his lip gently.

"You are so beautiful." Ezra was mesmerized with the woman he held tightly in his arms. "I have dreamt of this day for as long as I can remember."

"For me as well, Ezra. I do believe we were born for each other." She said as a whisper in his ear and stepped back from him. She untied her gown and let it hit the floor in a pile of soft satin. "I have waited long enough tonight for you to take me as your wife, talking is done."

He bowed backwards and put his hand to his heart. "Have mercy dear wife." He pleaded looking over her perfection. She walked away toward the bed swaying her hips teasing his senses. She heard his gear hit the floor behind her and then his boots. "I wasted time worrying when I could have been here with you, my hands touching every inch of your beautiful, delicious body. Shame on me." Ezra said, laying her gently onto the bed. She watched while he took his time undressing and admired every ripple in his stomach as he moved. His shoulders wide and thick moved easily as he climbed into the bed over her. "I owe you my full attention my lady, my wife." He kissed her lips. They were red and hot with desire. She reached between and touched his swollen member. He moved her hand away holding it in place on the bed as he placed kisses down her neck to her breasts. He gave each one the full attention they deserved.

"Ezra." She moaned raising her hips eagerly, hungering to receive him. His touch was so gentle, so loving it was hard not to give into the building emotions inside of her. She felt his tongue on her belly and the nibble he took just below her navel. Her hips rocked up when his tongue found her sweet spot and she sucked in air. "I can't wait." Asia cried.

"You don't have to; this is for you." Ezra said wickedly looking up at her then returned his attention to her swollen area. When she felt his hot breath upon her, she couldn't fight it any longer. Ezra entered her as she exploded, feeling her tightening around him. The sensation of her release built him up to his own climax.

******

A rapid knock on the door woke Ezra instantly.

It was Andrew. "Ezra, your father urgently sends for you."

"Yes, my lord. I will be right there." Ezra quickly dressed, stirring Asia from her sleep.

"What is it, Ezra?" She asked wrapping her robe around herself.

"I don't know." He kissed her. "My father calls." Ezra strapped his sword across his back and placed a dagger in his boot. Grayson followed Ezra to the front porch where Yori stood talking with Andrew and Charles.

"Ezra, two ridges over sits a barrage of the king's men. Their captain is Domminick. I want you to ride out and talk to him. Try to see if he will stay put for a while. We need time to get the people out of the area and on the road before his army moves in. Grayson will follow you in the shadows." Yori nodded at both his sons.

"Have Asia and Vada ride alongside the woods. Trust me, they are your best archers. Grayson and I will catch up with you as soon as we can." Ezra said, taking his father's extended forearm.

"Your horses are ready by the corral." Charles said as Ezra and Grayson passed by him.

"You're going to have my back without a sword?" Ezra asked his brother as he pulled on his riding gloves.

"Ezra if you have doubts about your protection by my hand or my loyalty you may feel free to choose another to ride with you." Grayson said as Ezra mounted his black stallion. Grayson rubbed the animal's nose with affection and looked up at Ezra for his answer. His decision not to carry a sword was final. What he did for Joe would forever be his reasoning. His marksmanship with the bow was with deadly accuracy and Ezra knew that.

"I have no doubts of your loyalty Gray, or the aim of your bow. I just miss seeing the blade on your back and the love for it in your eyes." Ezra said as Grayson stepped up onto his saddle and followed his brother into the darkness. Domminick watched a lone rider traveling on the horizon for a while. The sun was just starting to rise, and the light reflected the metal on the sword the man carried. Dom knew the man who approached was Ezra and decided to ride out to meet him.

"Ezra." Domminick greeted him.

"Domminick." Ezra returned his greeting. "This is my father in law's property. Why are the king's men camped out here?"

"We are here to seize this property Ezra, as per lord Samuel's orders. We are also to escort all peoples off said land and back to the castle for trial." Domminick said handing Ezra the poster. "Ezra, they know your families are leaving. The king has ordered the arrest of your father and lords Andrew and Charles for treason. If arrested, they will take their heads." Dom warned taking the poster back from Ezra.

"Come with us Dom." Ezra asked of his friend.

"I cannot come with you for the same reasons you cannot stay. My father is in the dungeon for failing to pay his taxes. I must work off his dept to free him as it is with most of the soldiers here with me." Dom waved his hand around indicating the army behind him.

"I pledge to you my friend; I will find a way to come back and free this kingdom from Idris's rule." Ezra said with his fist over his heart.

"I am counting on it." Dom said extending his arm. Ezra accepted. Dom turned his horse to leave. "I can hold off for two hours, Ezra. That's all I can do." He turned and looked once more at his friend. "Good luck, Ezra."

"You as well, my friend." Ezra urged his anxious horse into a steady pace back to the house.

******

Grayson rode his horse up beside his family's wagon. Barrett was sitting up front with their mother. Barrett was eating breakfast and telling stories to Clara when Grayson snuck up and snatched the biscuit from his brother's hand.

Barrett whipped his head from Grayson to his mother. "Mother? Did you see Grayson? He stole my biscuit!" Grayson laughed at the bewildered look on his little brother's face.

"What is it with you two and biscuits?" Clara asked, shaking her head.

"Hand me one for Vada, Barrett. She has not eaten yet this morning." Grayson said holding out his hand. "Where is father?" He asked his mother as he waited on Barrett.

"They rode ahead scouting for possible raiders." She nodded.

Grayson took the bread and smiled at Barrett. "She gets a bigger one?"

"Yes, I like her." Barrett replied sticking out his tongue. Grayson heard his mother scolding Barrett as he rode away.

"Good morning, my love. I bring you breakfast." Grayson quietly spoke as he rode up beside her.

"Good morning." She returned his greeting taking the bread. "Thank you, I am starving." They turned as Ezra and Asia rode up fast.

"There are raiders ahead! Father is fighting them as we speak." Ezra shouted and continued his horse onward in a full run. Clara watched as the four rode ahead of the wagons and fear plagued her.

"Barrett hop in the back and hide like I showed you." She said ushering him back with her hand.

******

Ezra drew his sword as he slid off his horse into the thick of the raiders. He kicked the first approaching man in the chest knocking him to the ground, then blocked the blade of the one coming up behind him and whirled slicing his neck ear to ear. Grayson slid the long knives from the sheaths at his mid back and made a path to his father. Yori was on his knees with a spear through his back, he stood and used his sword to break off the end continuing to fight.

"Vada!" Grayson shouted. She rode through the men knocking them out of the way with her horse. "Take him to mother." Grayson said as he helped Yori onto the animal. Ezra stood back to back with Charles and felt the whisp of an arrow as it whizzed past his ear and struck its intended target in the left eye. Ezra winked his thanks to Asia and turned to block the strike of another opponent. He glanced up to see Asia being pulled from her horse. Fear shot through him as he screamed her name. He couldn't get to her, but he saw Grayson was closer and shouted at him.

Grayson! Asia's down!" Ezra tried to push through but there were too many. He picked up a sword that lay on the ground and swung both in a slashing motion taking down three men at once. "Asia!" He screamed. When Grayson reached her, she was underneath a man squirming to free herself. Asia pulled an arrow from her quiver, rammed it into his neck and created a gaping wound with the tip of the arrow. Blood flowed out of his neck staining her dress and the ground.

Grayson pulled her out from underneath the dead man. "Are you good?" He asked her and she nodded. Ezra saw her head pop up and was relieved.

"Ezra we've got to get to Andrew. They are boxing him in." Charles shouted over the clanking of swords.

"Asia! Mount up and get to that hill. Your father needs support!" Ezra shouted. Grayson tossed her up on her horse just as he was attacked. Grayson threw an uppercut into the man's jaw then cut the femoral arteries on the legs of his assailant. Ezra pulled his dagger from his boot and thew it in one smooth motion striking a man between the eyes. Grayson pulled Ezra's blade from the dead man's skull and plunged it into the heart of another who had his aim on Charles. Vada rode back fast with ladies Sara and Marcy. "Ladies! On the hilltop with Asia and make it rain!" Ezra ordered. "Alright my lord lets push back to Andrew," He said to Charles. "Grayson push them back!" Ezra shouted. "We're heading to Andrew. The ladies are on the hill!" Grayson looked up to see them all with readied bows. "Asia! On your command." Ezra yelled as he swung both blades in a circle on each side. Tucking one under his arm he swung the other around slicing at one's middle spilling his insides. Then swung the other blade around doing the same to another. He felt pain in his arm and turned to see that the cause was a ten year old boy with a sword that was too heavy for him. The boy was frightened and backed up when Ezra reached for him. Ezra heard Asia give the order to fire and pulled the boy in close to him tossing down the blade the boy held. "Be still boy!" Ezra growled when he tried to wiggle away from Ezra. Arrows whistled past them picking out their targets and felled the men which were aimed. When the arrows stopped none of the raiders were left but the boy. Ezra held his arm tightly until he was joined by his family.

"What are you going to do with him?" Andrew asked and pointed a sword under the boy's chin, raising it up.

"Set him free." Ezra said looking down at the boy. "You will go home. Tell your people what has happened here today. Tell them how you were defeated by us and that we demand safe passage to our destination, or the same fate will fall upon them. Understood?" The boy nodded and Ezra let him go. He ran to the edge of the woods and then turned to look at Ezra and bowed respectively.

Asia saw blood drop from Ezra's fingertips and tore a section from the bottom of her skirt and wrapped it around the wound on Ezra's upper arm.

"We should get back to the wagons." Charles said mounting his horse. Andrew turned to retrieve his horse and felt a sharp pain in his side. When he placed his hand there and pulled it back it was covered in blood. Quickly, he wiped it away before anyone noticed. His horse was standing by the edge of the woods, slowly he walked over to where it stood. Reaching down for the reins he didn't see the rattler that was curled up by a rock and it bit him on the hand. He cried out in frustration and cut its head off with his sword. His horse, spooked by the snake, reared up. Grayson grasped the reins as the horse trotted past him. Andrew walked back over to where his wife stood and smiled at her.

"Wife I may be in a bit of a predicament." He said to Sara and showed her the wound on his side as well as the bite.

"Yes, you might be indeed." Sara said with concern. "We need to get you back to the wagon so I can add medicine to your wound and drain the venom from the bite." She looked to Grayson and Ezra for help.

"I can get on my own horse by myself wife." Andrew said with frustration. Grayson walked the horse over to him and held it still.

"Well, do it so we can get you back to the wagon." She fussed back at him and saw blood gush out of his side when he slowly mounted his horse. The reaction she saw on Grayson's face when he watched Andrew was what she feared herself. Her husband might not make it.

******

"Lord Ezra, your mother requests your presence at her wagon." One of the wagon masters said riding up to Ezra and Charles. The man bowed then turned to ride back to his station. Ezra looked at Charles with surprise which caused Charles to chuckle.

"You have earned the title, my lord." Charles nodded.

"Stop. I am not a lord." Ezra frowned. "I have no standing."

"Ezra, word has spread of your leadership in battle. With no loss of life among your people you have earned the title. You are a natural leader." Charles said watching his words process with Ezra. "Go see to your mother's needs I will keep watch here until your return." Ezra looked at Charles but did not say anything. He turned his horse and rode back down the wagon train. The air was changing, becoming cooler. The leaves are just starting to bring on their autumn glory. A breeze blew across Ezra's neck, and he flipped up his collar. He didn't realize that the look made him look more like the lord they professed him to be.

"Mother, you called for me?" He asked, riding up beside their wagon. She was inside with Yori tending to his wounds.

"Your father will heal. It will take time, but he will heal. Your wife's father, however, will not. The wound he received in battle was a fatal one and the reaction from the snake bite is severe. He is having trouble breathing and is in shock. You should be with Asia." She said glancing up at her son as she worked on Yori's wound. "I think we should camp here tonight son."

"It is too dangerous to stay here tonight. We must travel a few more miles before we stop. As soon as you are finished with father start the wagons. Barrett can sit with Father and shout if he needs you." Ezra said and rode toward Asia. "James," Ezra stopped his horse at his wagon. "We are two swordsmen down. Keep yours handy, we will need your blade."

"Aye, my lord." James pounded his chest with his fist and bowed. Ezra nodded then rode to his wife. Grayson was standing outside the wagon Andrew lay in holding Vada. Sara was bandaging Andrew's side and Asia was tending to his swollen hand where he was bit. He was conscious but barely.

"Ezra," Andrew said through gasps of air. "I'm sorry lad I don't think I will be making the journey after all."

"Andrew, stop talking save your strength." Sara fussed. A tear snuck down her cheek. She knew no matter what she did he was not going to make it.

"My girls are in your charge now. Yours and Grayson's." Andrew mumbled as he drifted off. Asia looked at Ezra sadness filling her eyes.

"Grayson, we are moving forward a few miles until dusk. It is too dangerous to stay here." Ezra said and Asia interrupted him.

"Moving forward? Ezra, my father cannot stand the ride." She said with disbelief.

"We don't have a choice, Asia. We can go slower, but we still must move." Ezra said tilting his head sideways looking in her eyes hoping she saw his sadness for her.

"A word, Ezra?" Grayson asked and waited for Ezra to step down from his horse. They walked away from the wagon to talk. "He won't make it through the night. Can we not wait and camp here tonight?"

"Andrew would not let me wait on his account. I know it sounds heartless, but I have other people to worry about not just him. Our own father lay just steps away from us in their wagon, yet I show no special treatment for him. All these people are counting on us to keep them alive. All of them, Gray." Ezra climbed back on his horse. "I would appreciate if you would ride ahead and scout for a place to camp for the night."

"I will do as you ask." Grayson nodded understanding his position. Ezra rode over to where Asia sat in the wagon next to her father.

"Asia, I will be back soon, I promise." He touched her chin and leaned in to kiss her lips. "Lady Sara, I will have you a driver so you may stay with lord Andrew." She nodded, not taking her eyes from her husband's shallow breaths. Ezra turned his head when he heard the wagons starting to move. He rode over to where his father lay in the back of their wagon before meeting with Charles. He was awake but in pain and the bumpy ride of the wagon wasn't helping. "I am sorry Father, but I felt we should leave this area as soon as possible."

"It is the right thing, Ezra. How is Andrew? Your mother told me she feared the worst." Yori said trying to sit up.

"He may not make it to camp, Father. Grayson is scouting for a place now. Hopefully, we can stop before he passes." Ezra said thinking of Asia his heart feeling heavy with grief for her.

"He wouldn't want you to wait, Ezra." Yori saw the doubt in his son's face. "Bring my horse. I cannot stand this ride any longer."

"Yori, you stay put." Clara fussed looking back at her husband.

"Wife, you have hit every rock and hole on this trail. I stand a better chance of survival on the back of my horse." Yori argued back to her.

"Ezra, can Barrett ride with you a bit? It'll give my ears a rest." Clara asked pleading with her eldest son. Barrett had been telling stories since they left, and she needed a break.

"Come Barrett, let's check on lord Charles." Ezra said, catching him as he jumped from the wagon. "Father, are you sure about riding your horse?" He asked watching him wince in pain climbing onto the animal.

"Trust me this is better." Yori said with a sigh. They rode ahead to where Charles was leading the train.

"Yori." Charles nodded glad to see his friend.

James rode up to them acknowledging all three. "My lord Ezra, a family sits to the west just a ways and are asking permission to join our journey."

"I will talk with them." Ezra said and followed James to where the family waited.

Yori whipped his head around to Charles and looked at him with humor. "Lord Ezra?"

"He's earned the title. Ezra assumed leadership in that battle. He fought with two swords, Yori. Your son is the best swordsman I have ever seen." Charles looked at his friend. "Even better than you."

******

"Lord Ezra, this is Drake, he is a blacksmith by trade." James introduced.

"My lord," Drake bowed. "My wife Sadie and our son Cole." Barrett waved at the boy who seemed to be his age.

"Can you yield a sword master Drake?" Ezra asked.

"No, my lord, but I can make them, and my wife, she is a seamstress. We are homeless now, our business and homestead taken by the crown. My wife and I would like the opportunity to start new with your family." Drake humbly asked.

"Say yes, Ezra." Barrett whispered elbowing his brother.

"This is my brother, Barrett, who will have to walk back if he elbows me again. He looked down at Barrett and raised an eyebrow at him. "Welcome," He said returning his attention to Drake. "James show them where they can pull in." James nodded and headed to the end of the train.

"Thank you." Drake said to Ezra as they followed James.

Barrett waved at Cole as they left. "I bet we'll be best friends."

"I have no doubts little brother. Let's see if Grayson has found a camp site yet." Ezra said as they returned. Grayson was talking to Charles and their father upon their return.

"It's about a thirty-minute ride from here. There's a little stream with good water and fish to eat. It will be perfect for the night." Grayson said nodding at his brothers when they approached.

"That's good. I think that's all your father has left in him today." Charles said, noticing the blood seeping through the bandage.

******

When they reached the stream Andrew's breaths were drawing farther and farther apart. His arm and neck were very swollen and he had nearly bled out. Sara had been working diligently trying to stop the bleeding, but she knew in her heart she would not be continuing this journey with her husband. Asia held the packing against her father's side, not willing to give up.

"Nate!" Sara shouted at a young boy running by.

"Yes, my lady." He bowed.

"Go tell Ezra and Grayson to come to my wagon posthaste. Run Nate!" Sara shouted. Clara heard Sara's hastened command and ran to her pulling her skirts up careful not to trip over them.

"Sara?" She said looking over the top of the wagon. Sara glanced over at her friend and shook her head. She was exhausted from the struggle of trying to save him. She sat up and watched Andrew take his last breath. Sara moved Asia's hands away from her father's side and tried to smile at her daughter.

"He's gone." Sara said as she watched her daughters grasp the idea that their father had passed. Grayson rode up and hurried down from his horse. He wrapped Vada in his arms as she wept. Asia looked for Ezra. He stood at the foot of the wagon and held out his hand for her. Sara kissed her husband goodbye and laid a blanket over him.

Ezra helped her down from the wagon. I am sorry Mother Sara." She smiled at him but couldn't speak. Clara took her hand and led her away. Asia looked around frantically realizing she hadn't seen her little sister in a while.

"Asia, what is wrong?" Vada asked watching her look underneath the wagon.

"Where is Jenna?" Asia asked with panic as she looked at Vada.

******

"PaPa! Why did you leave me?" Jenna cried out. "I need you PaPa!" She placed her little hands over her heart in fists. She fell to her knees and screamed. "My heart hurts so much!" She laid her head on a soft tuff of grass and looked at the sky. "Can you see me, Father?" She asked through the pain.

"He will always be with you little one." A soft voice whispered in the dark. Jenna sat up quickly and looked around at the shadows.

"Who is there?" Jenna asked startled. A black wolf slowly walked up and laid down in front of her.

"Don't worry child I will not hurt you." Jenna heard the wolf with her mind not her ears.

"I wouldn't care if you did." Jenna pouted and threw a stone at the closest tree.

"Sweet girl, I know your pain. I promise it will ease with time." The wolf tried to ease her sorrow.

"That is what all grownups say. I don't believe you." Jenna glared at the wolf, then gently the anger fell away, and the tears began once more.

"One day Jenna, you will meet someone that will be in pain like you are today. He will need your help and your love." The wolf tilted her head to the side and softly growled.

"Have you ever lost anyone?" Jenna asked and crawled over to the wolf curling up next to her. The wolf's fur was warm and soft. The comfort she needed so desperately.

"I lost my daughter and my mate. It was a very long time ago, but I still feel the loss. That's how I know you will be ok." The wolf whispered as Jenna lay quietly and with the comfort of the wolf's heartbeat.

"Why does it hurt so much?" Jenna whispered softly.

"Because you loved your father so very much and now that he is gone your heart holds your pain." The wolf licked the tears from the side of Jenna's face. "You will forever carry his memories Jenna and someday they won't be so painful to recall.

******

Vada walked beside Grayson as they looked for Jenna. The woods were being searched by everyone from the train. They cried out her name throughout the night.

"I don't know how we're going to hear her cry with all the other voices echoing through the night." Grayson growled.

"Vada." A voice rang inside her ears. Vada froze listening for it again. Grayson started to speak, and Vada put her finger to her lips. "Vada, she is with me. She is safe." They heard the faint howl of a wolf. The sound pulled at her heart, and she knew she was to follow.

"She's with the wolf." Vada said and headed in the direction they heard the howl. As they got closer, the wolf growled softly letting them know they were close. They saw Jenna curled up next to the wolf sleeping. Grayson slowly reached down and picked her up. "Thank you for keeping her safe." Vada said sitting on her legs in front of the wolf. She looked the wolf in the eyes and felt a familiar connection. "Why do I feel like I know you?" Vada asked. The wolf licked her face and seemed to smile at her. When she laid her head on Vada's shoulder Vada hugged her gently. Grayson watched the wolf's affection to his wife and wondered if this wasn't the same wolf they saw their wedding night. She pulled away from Vada and trotted away into the night. Grayson held out his hand to help Vada stand. Vada looked at Grayson, her eyes full of questions. "I don't understand."

"Come, sweetheart, let's take Jenna back to your mother." Grayson said taking her hand.

"My mother? Grayson, it felt as though she was my mother." Vada said looking back where the wolf once stood.

When Sara saw Grayson holding her daughter she ran to him. "Oh, Jenna," She cried. "I thought I had lost you too."

Grayson handed Jenna to her mother then took Vada in his arms. "I don't know how to help you through this, but just to be here for you." Grayson whispered to her.

******

Vada dreamed of her ambulant. She watched as wolves pushed through the crack, growling and snapping their teeth. She tossed in her sleep as the ambulant broke. The wolves disappeared and in their stead was a beautiful woman with long black hair. She walked toward Vada as a mist fell around them. Suddenly, the woman was face to face with her. Vada gasped in her sleep waking Grayson.

"It has begun daughter." The woman spoke and looked at Vada's arms. Vada looked down to see that she was covered in fur and felt the incredible urge to run. Grayson touched her arm when she started throwing herself around.

"Vada," He shook her. "Wake up." Her eyes popped open and she examined her arms and touched her face with urgency. She reached for her ambulant. It was gone. She looked at Grayson with calmness.

"I don't think I'm supposed to have it anymore." She snuggled up to Grayson. "Our lives are about to change Grayson; I am just not sure how."

"Whatever it is my love we shall face it together." Grayson pulled her in closer and they drifted back to sleep.

******

Asia couldn't leave her father's grave. The others were already heading down the trail, but she couldn't bring herself to ride away. Her eyes were swollen from a night of crying and the new tears that welled up burned a salty reminder of her grief. Memories of his warm smile and gentle voice flooded her mind and threatened to overwhelm her. "Father, how are we supposed to do this without you?" She asked and laid a flower down on the freshly turned soil. She felt Ezra's arms slip around her waist and his head rested on top of hers. "My feet are rooted here, my love. I cannot seem to make them turn and lead me away. I command them but they listen not." She sniffed and smiled slightly up at her husband.

"I can't imagine what you are going through right now Asia. How can I help?" Ezra asked and kissed the top of her head.

"Pick me up and put me on my horse. Ezra, I plead with you my husband that is the only way my body will leave his grave." Asia said wiping the new tears away. Ezra felt one of them splatter on his hand and picked her up in his arms. He looked into her big beautiful sad eyes and kissed her lips before sliding her into her saddle. He took the reins to her horse and then mounted his own. She did not look back when they left. She knew if she did, she would go back. "Ezra, I'm going to check on my mother. Go tend to your duties." She managed to smile. "Go on, I promise I am ok." Asia said when he gave her a doubtful look. Ezra watched her making sure she would ride forward and not back to her father's grave. When he was satisfied, after a while he rode to find his father.

******

"Grayson," Yori turned to his son as they rode alongside the wagons. "What did Jack whisper to you in the prison when he pulled you into the cell door?"

"It didn't make any sense to me really." Grayson said shrugging his shoulders. "He said 'You are of my blood. Do not let the wolf take your mind.'" Grayson noticed his father shift in his saddle and the side of his face twitch.

"Your right it does not make sense but coming from a mad mind it's hard to tell what he meant." Yori dismissed it with a smile. Grayson knew his father well enough to know it meant something to him. But he left it alone for now. Grayson looked back behind him when he heard the stallion trot up. Ezra sat tall in the saddle and looked the part of a lord. Grayson smiled at his brother when he approached.

"The season is changing fast." Ezra said with a shiver.

"Aye, I feel it in my old bones." Yori said looking up at the sky. "The way those clouds look we may be in for storms tonight."

"Yori!" Clara shouted at him as she was passing by with the wagon. "Come get this son of yours before my ears fall off."

"Telling tall tales, is he?" Yori asked, riding up alongside her.

"As lovely as it is that he has an imagination, it has been a long day of nonstop stories. Nonstop, Yori." Her voice changed pitch, and he knew she was ready for some peace.

"Come along Barrett, ride with me a bit." Yori chuckled as the boy jumped at his father from the seat of the wagon.

"Father how much longer until we get there? I have been thinking about what it will be like, living by the water. Will there be sharks? Do you think I could ride one?" Barrett continued with a new audience.

"Enjoy, my love." Clara giggled. "He is all yours."

"Do you think that Ezra and Grayson could ride a shark? They are bigger than I am. I bet they could. Will there be eagles? I heard they like the water. They like fish don't they father? I think they do." Barrett looked up at Yori and waited for an answer.

Yori chuckled. "Barrett, we should be there in a couple of days. There probably are sharks but you would not be able to ride them without becoming their dinner and I don't think your brothers would want to try riding a shark. Yes, you will see eagles and yes, they love fish. Now I need you to help me find a suitable place to camp."

******

"Vada, your ambulant is missing." Sara mentioned to Vada as she and Grayson sat down for supper.

"I lost it in the woods when we were searching for Jenna." Vada said with sadness. "I know it was my mother's, but the wolf made me feel at ease about it. Like it was supposed to happen." Vada noticed Sara's lips tighten.

"My lady, is there something Vada should know about her mother?" Grayson asked. "Why does this ambulant other than being a possession of her mother's seem to be a worry to others? And what of this wolf that seems to be everywhere we are now?"

"I know very little of your parents, Vada. Lady Clara brought you to live with us after your family was lost in a fire. I know they were important in their community and well-loved but that is all I know. As for the wolf, I am grateful of her care for Jenna, but it is probably just a coincidence." Grayson started to speak again, and Vada touched his arm. She knew she would not learn anymore, at least tonight. Jenna ran up behind Grayson and put her arms around his neck.

"I think you have a new friend." Vada smiled when Grayson pulled her sister around into his lap and tickled her. A sudden chill swept over them with a ghostly bite to it. Sara wrapped her shawl tighter around herself. Everyone was quiet. This wasn't a normal fall breeze this was something else. Grayson stood and looked around.

He saw Ezra at the edge of the meadow looking toward the wood line in front of them.

"Vada, I am going to see Ezra. Keep your bow close. Something doesn't feel right." Grayson kissed Vada and headed toward his brother. Ezra bent down and broke off a stem of wheat. A breeze whipped around him, and he heard his name whispered in it. There was a figure just inside the trees, very faint and transparent. Ezra watched it intensely as did the spirit he and felt an overwhelming desire to follow the entity into the woods. He heard Grayson and his father's footsteps behind him but did not turn. His gaze stayed fixed on the one across the meadow.

"Those woods give a man cause for the hair to stand up on his neck." Yori said standing next to Ezra.

"Have you ever been here before?" Ezra asked of his father.

"No, I haven't. I don't have any knowledge of these woods being here. The maps I studied only showed meadows and valleys here forward." Yori flipped his collar up as a chilling breeze blew around them.

Grayson ran his hand over the top of the wheat. "The wind blows but does not move the leaves or the grass. What's in those woods are not of this world." Ezra walked forward feeling it drawing him. It spoke his name again. Grayson tried to follow his brother but couldn't. He felt himself being pushed backwards with little pulses of electrical waves. "Ezra! We can't follow!" Grayson shouted but his brother could not hear him. Grayson looked at Yori with concern then they both saw what Ezra saw. Ezra continued to walk toward the entity, strangely he felt no fear. A fog was rolling out from the trees into the meadow and inhaled Ezra as he strolled into it.

"I don't like this. I can't see him." Grayson said pushing against the barrier that kept him from his brother. When the fog rolled in to where they stood a figure suddenly appeared in front of him.

A cold boney hand touched Grayson's face. It was a touch so cold it burned his cheek. "Do not be afraid." She whispered. Her face was beautiful on the side she showed to him, the other side was of bone and death. "Your brother shall return. He has been chosen."

"Chosen for what?" Grayson asked.

******

"Ezra." A ghostly figure smiled at him when he entered the edge of the woods. "We have been waiting a long time for you." The entity took on a human like appearance and seemed to be about his father's age. He wore the attire of royalty and upon his head was a crown of which Ezra had never seen before. Elegant and regal with dragons breathing fire on either side to a point where sat an opal gem. A sword lay flat across his forearm and the hilt the king held was magnificent. Written words glowed in a blue hue down the length of the blade. A dragon curled around to form the hilt and were of Ezra's colors of silver and black.

Ezra bowed instantly, respectfully. "Your majesty."

"Ezra, you have been chosen." The king said as other kings and queens for a thousand years faintly stood behind him. "Rise son of Yori." The king handed Ezra the dragon sword. "This now belongs to you, the new King of Dragons."

Ezra quickly looked from the sword to the king. "Your majesties, my blood carries no weight of royalty. How can I serve as king?" Ezra questioned.

"You were chosen." All the voices echoed sounding like thunder, and frightened crows flew from the trees cawing warnings.

******

Grayson and Yori saw the explosion of crows fly from woods with the roaring sound which echoed through the meadow.

Charles rode up to where they stood and dismounted his horse. "Well, that looks ominous."

"Ezra is in there." Yori said not taking his eyes from the spot his son disappeared.

"And why are the both of you still standing here?" Charles asked, holding the reins to his nervous horse tightly in his hands. The animal wanted no part of this haunted ambiance.

"She won't let us pass." Grayson said with his arms crossed.

"She?" Charles asked, raising an eyebrow. Yori pointed at the entity. "Oh, yes, I see." Charles said, nodding toward her when she looked his way. "Are neither one of you about to wet yourselves over this nightmare?" Charles asked looking straight ahead avoiding the spirit.

"Yes." Yori answered calmly.

"Down both legs." Grayson agreed.

******

"When you leave here you will carry the knowledge and understanding of those before you. It will not all make sense now, but will as you live." The king spoke and laid his hand upon Ezra's shoulder. "There will be a cave by the coast for your people to take refuge out of the storm that is coming. Your kingship will be established there and not questioned." The king bowed to Ezra. "You are now and forever more King Ezra lord and master of dragons."

"Long live King Ezra!" The entities echoed.

"Ezra, King Idris's men are closing in on your people. You must move them through the woods. I promise you will have safe passage." The king warned and his appearance vanished with all those behind him. Ezra ran to the edge of the woods and whistled for his horse. The stallion galloped past Grayson with no fear of what lay ahead, only a need to serve.

******

"Where is Ezra?" Asia asked walking up behind them. They all pointed toward the woods beyond the fog. Asia looked at them as she walked past.

"Asia, I don't think you can…" Grayson started to say as the ghostly woman bowed to her letting her pass. Grayson frowned at the entity.

"Queen." She whispered gesturing Asia and followed her into the fog. Whatever was holding them back was now gone and Grayson began to walk forward. He stopped when he heard a horse snort and hooves hitting the earth.

Ezra parted the fog as he and Asia rode the stallion toward them.

"Father, we must get everyone through the woods. Idris's men are quickly approaching." Ezra said with urgency. "Grayson find James and guard the rear. Keep pushing them forward. Tell them not to fear we shall have safe passage." Grayson nodded to his brother.

Charles slapped Yori on the back as they turned to leave. "My friend, I think you have just been outranked."

"Yes, it would seem so." Yori grinned back at Charles. Yori climbed aboard his wagon and took the reins from Clara. "We've got to travel swiftly; company is fast approaching."

Ezra rode down the line to Sara's wagon. "Vada, I need you and Asia in the shadows and bring up the rear with Grayson and James." Ezra helped Asia down from his horse. "Lady Sara, keep the line tight. We must move quickly."

"What about me, Ezra?" Jenna asked, feeling left out.

"Do you have your bow, lady Jenna?' Ezra asked.

"I do!" She picked it up and slid her quiver onto her back.

"You must keep watch to the side that none sneak past your sisters." He smiled when he saw the determined look on her face. "Jenna, you may see scary things when traveling through the woods. Do not be afraid."

"I am not afraid." Jenna said sticking her nose in the air.

"That a girl." Ezra said then rode on down the line. "Keep close to the wagon in front of you. We must move with haste to pass through the woods." Ezra shouted with urgency. When he reached the last wagon Grayson was riding up from scouting for the barrage.

"They are riding fast, Ezra." Grayson warned.

Ezra pulled his sword and Grayson noticed the writing down the blade.

"What happened in there Ez? Grayson asked, nodding toward the woods.

"A lot of things I don't understand." Ezra looked down at the sword. "They gave me this. He said they have been waiting for me."

"That blade is a king's sword." Grayson said with recognition.

"The one with whom I spoke to was a king. He handed me this sword; said I was to lead the people and would be named king of dragons." Ezra shrugged. "I guess we will find out." Raindrops smacked his shoulder and he looked to the sky. "Ride up to father and tell him he must pick up the pace." Ezra said to his brother and watched as Domminick and his men were gaining ground. One by one the wagons disappeared into the fog ridden woods. A breeze whipped the mane on Ezra's stallion as he waited by the wood line. The fog rolled around him giving them a ghostly appearance. Domminick stopped at the edge of the meadow and looked at Ezra. The stallion stomped impatiently trying to follow the wagons. Ezra turned the horse around to look once more at his friend. He raised his sword high in the air and for a moment Dom thought he saw a king's crown on Ezra's head. When Ezra rode into the trees light flashed across the meadow blinding Domminick and his men. A burst of energy swept across the meadow knocking them from their saddles. When Dom regained his senses the woods ahead of them were gone and so was Ezra. Confident that Dom couldn't follow, and they were safe he slowed down the train. Ezra rode up along the wagons checking on everyone as he made his way up to his father. Asia was riding beside them chatting with his mother.

"Asia, we need to talk." Ezra said seriously. He led his horse away and she followed.

"Ezra are you ok?" Asia asked concerned about his serious behavior.

"Our lives are about to change dramatically." He pulled his sword and showed it to her. The writing down the blade was lit with a blue hue.

"It is a beautiful sword." She said touching the cool steel. "What does it say?"

"The King of Dragons, Merciful with Truth and Honor." Ezra explained everything to her then looked into her eyes. "You will be my queen, if...you so choose."

"I choose to be with you, no matter our titles, Ezra." Asia said leaning closer to kiss him.

******

Sara pulled her wagon to the side when she saw Vada, seemingly sick, standing beside her horse. "Vada, sweetheart, are you ok?" Vada's eyes, dark as a starless night rose to meet Sara's. Holding her stomach in pain, she let Sara guide her to the wagon.

"Where is Grayson?" She asked as she lay down.

"Mother, I can find him." Jenna said climbing into the back of the wagon.

"No, Jenna." Sara said shaking her head.

"I can do it, Mother, please." Jenna begged knowing they needed her help. Vada cried out in pain and Sara looked at Jenna again and sighed.

"OK, take Vada's horse and find Grayson. Come right back, Jenna." Sara said sternly.

"I will." Jenna said and climbed out of the wagon onto Vada's horse. Sara watched her ride away then brought her attention back to Vada when she whimpered. Sara looked up when she heard a growl from the edge of the path.

"Salora, you took the ambulant too soon. She's going to change before Grayson is ready." Sara said with irritation pinching her eyebrows together. The wolf transformed and she stepped up to the wagon.

She lovingly touched her daughter on the forehead. "She's burning up." Salora said and lifted Vada's lip. "Her canines are still normal. She should be ok in a little bit. You don't have much farther to travel Sara." Salora said and smiled at Vada. "She is so beautiful."

"Like her mother." Sara said politely. "Salora, come with us. Let your daughter know you."

"I wish that I could, but this is the last time I will see her. I cannot travel where you go. When you leave the woods, they will disappear and so will I." Salora kissed her daughter's cheek. "Thank you for taking care of her Sara." Sara looked up to see horses riding up and when she looked back for Salora she was gone.

"Vada?" Grayson said sliding off his horse and climbing into the wagon. "What happened?" He asked with worry, looking up at Sara.

"I don't know. She was getting sick when I drove by and was crying out with stomach pains. After I helped her into the wagon she lost consciousness." Sara said looking over her shoulder for Salora.

"Vada, sweetheart." He put her head in his lap and brushed her hair away from her face. Vada opened her eyes slowly and rose up startled.

"What happened?" Vada asked looking at Grayson and Sara for answers.

"That's what we would like to know." Grayson asked cupping her chin with his hand and looking into her eyes.

"I don't know. The last thing I remember was sitting on my horse." Vada moved her shoulders around and placed her hand on her stomach when the movement presented soreness there. "I do feel like I have fell down a mountain side."

"Would you stay in the wagon with Lady Sara for a while? For me?" Grayson pleaded when he saw her look at him with aggravation.

"Grayson." Jenna said looking wide eyed at the tree line. There were ghostly figures lined up alongside the path.

The one that came forward and pointed to the road ahead, Grayson noticed as the same entity from before. His face began to burn where her boney fingers had touched him. She had his attention. "You must go."

Grayson nodded to her and looked at Jenna. "Get in the wagon Jenna." He helped her over to the wagon and tied the horse to the back of it. "Ok Sara, start them up." Grayson said as he mounted his horse. Vada looked back at him and he winked. She whispered the words I love you and blew him a kiss.

******

Grayson saw Ezra at the edge of the woods and rode up to meet him. Ezra was looking at the heavy clouds that loomed above them. They had been traveling through the dense thicket of trees for what seemed to be hours. It was hard to distinguish the time of day with no sun or stars to reference by.

"How is Vada?" Ezra asked as Grayson stopped beside him.

"I don't know if she is sick or it's just this direful unfavorable forest. How much longer do you suppose we will be in this ghostly hollow?" Grayson asked as he looked behind the proceeding wagons.

"I am not sure, hopefully not too much longer. Those clouds are holding a lot of rain and or snow. The air is getting cold enough it could go either way." Ezra said as a large drop splattered on the top of his horse's head. The stallion turned his head and looked at Ezra wild eyed. "It was not me." Ezra laughed.

"How do you know we are even going in the right direction?" Grayson inquired shifting his weight in the saddle. He had been sitting far too long.

Ezra pulled his sword out of the sheath on his back and held it out in front of him with the flat side up. As he moved the blade from side to side the light of the wording would dim when off the path directed. "I just don't know how much longer we will travel." Ezra looked back at their father sitting tall in the wagon beside his wife. "I feel Father is upset with me over my future kingship of our people."

"I will not coddle you with words of comfort whether Father has frustrations of your advancements or not. You must talk to him yourself, Ezra." Grayson smiled at his brother. "It suits you though. You have always had the mannerisms of a king." Ezra smiled back at Grayson and rode up beside Yori.

"Father," Ezra nodded with respect.

"Ezra, do you know how much longer we must drudge through this gloomy thicket?" Clara asked her eldest.

"Mother, I don't know. Hopefully soon. I understand the wariness of everyone and the need to rest." Ezra hesitated a moment then looked at Yori. "Father, are you angry with the turn of events that has put me in position or just with me?"

"Son, I am not angry at all. Your impending kingship is well warranted. You have been conditioned all your life for this moment although we had no clue of your future." Yori smiled at Ezra. "Angry? No, my son. I am proud."

"Thank you, Father." There was relief written across Ezra's face. His father's approval meant more than Yori would ever know. Ezra saw Asia and rode to her. "Ride with me." He said and helped her across to sit behind him. Her horse was tied to the back of the wagon, and they rode ahead of everyone.

She wrapped her arms around his waist and squeezed. "I have not seen much of you of late."

"I know. I am sorry. I thought we might ride ahead together to see if we might see an end to this never-ending fog and gloom." Ezra looked over his shoulder at her and smiled.

"It is a bit depressing. What do you think is on the other side?" She asked with curiosity.

"The cove. Home." He paused. "So, I was told. But what I didn't learn is how long it would take to arrive. The storm that looms overhead is a concern. I hope that we reach the cave they spoke of before it breaks."

"Look, Ezra, ahead." Asia pointed. An entity stood before them, a beautiful crown upon her head and she wore a gown that flowed with the moving fog. Obviously, a queen by the way she held herself with grace and dignity while waiting for them to meet her.

"Your majesty." Ezra said as he and Asia dismounted. He bowed and Asia curtsied.

"Your grace," She spoke but her lips moved not. "You have come to the end of your journey through this passage. Stop your people and feed them. The freezing rain will begin shortly, and you will seek shelter in the cave. Changes will begin within that will forever change you and the world." She stood to the side and gestured with her hand to the road that led out of the woods. Ezra bowed again to her and he and Asia walked to the edge of the trees. It was a meadow much like the one they left from. Thunder rolled overhead shaking the ground. Sprinkles of rain lightly fell and froze on the grass giving it a glass like appearance. Yori's wagon was first to cross the line over into the meadow.

"May I suggest a break, son? The children are tired and hungry." Yori suggested.

"Yes, I agree." Ezra said and turned to Asia. "Would you take the stallion and ride down the train and announce a short break once outside of the woods?" He assisted her into the saddle and watched her ride back inside the fog.

******

Grayson walked his horse beside Sara's wagon with Vada by his side. Jenna rode on his horse pretending she was a princess and waving politely to everyone around her. Grayson slipped his arm around Vada's waist and kissed her cheek.

"My wife, are you feeling better?" Grayson asked with concern. She still looked pale.

"I don't even remember being ill, Grayson." She answered with a sigh.

"We have reached the end of our travel through this grim and ghostly timber. Ezra stands on the other side in a meadow with Yori. We are to camp for a spell before completing our journey to the cove." Asia smiled giving them the news.

"Tis good to hear, Asia. We can all use a meal and a rest." Vada said happily squeezing Grayson's hand.

"There is a storm ready to spill so it won't be a long rest." Asia warned.

******

Ezra awaited his wife's return on the outskirts of the meadow and together they watched the last wagon ride out of the darkening woods. The fog receded, the crows returned to the trees and the humming of voices sang out for the implosion of the woods they had traveled through. As quickly as the blink of an eye it was gone, no evidence it had ever existed but the memories of those that traveled through it. Ezra pulled Asia in close to him and kissed her lovingly.

"I wish I had a private moment with you." He said running his hand down her back to her bottom.

"I as well, husband." She giggled tugging his beard. Lightening splintered overhead that unleashed a thunderous roar. It fueled Ezra's passion but there was nowhere to go. Wind whipped around them lifting Asia's hair and tossing it around them. Lightning flashed again and again above them. The thunder rumbled the ground under their feet. Asia moaned in his ear and he gently pushed her away.

"Asia, you are making it very difficult to stop and as much as I want to lay you down at this moment under this storm I cannot."

******

"What are you doing Cole?" Barrett asked as he watched his friend poke a hole with the stick he held.

"There is something in that hole." Cole said concentrating on the creature living inside. "I saw something move."

"Was it a snake?" Barrett asked squatting down beside Cole.

"I don't think so. I think it was a big ol spider." Cole's eyes widened as he turned. Barrett fell backwards and scrambled to his feet. "What's the matter with you?" Cole asked standing. Barrett saw that the spider in question was riding on the end of the stick Cole held. His face went pale with panic. Cole looked from Barrett to the spider and stuck it closer to him.

Barrett stuck up both hands. "Keep it back, Cole. It has most definitely escaped from the haunted forest. It will eat us!"

"It's just a tiny spider, Barrett." Cole said looking at it closely. "There's probably more spider holes all over." Fear froze Barrett where he stood. Wide eyed he looked around his feet hunting for any more of those thousand eyed monsters. Cole looked at Barrett with confusion. He never knew anyone afraid of spiders.

"Please find Grayson." Barrett asked shaking.

"Ok, Barrett. I'm sorry." Cole said and felt bad that he teased him. Barrett watched as Cole ran back to find his brother. He tried to move but he would then imagine a spider jumping on him and couldn't bear it. He sighed when he saw Grayson start his way. A tear snuck down his cheek, but he didn't care.

"What's the matter Barrett?" Grayson asked kneeling in front of his brother.

"Spiders, they're everywhere. I don't want to be here Grayson. I want to go home." Grayson stood and picked Barrett up.

"I didn't know he was so afraid of them." Cole said looking up at Grayson.

"He'll be ok, Cole." Grayson assured him. He carried Barrett back to the wagon and handed him to Clara. "Spiders." Grayson winked at his mother.

"Oh, I see." She said rocking her son in her lap.

"You shouldn't coddle him, Clara." Yori frowned. "How will he ever get over it if you keep babying him?"

"Probably the same time you get over your fear of snakes." Clara smiled looking at him out of the corner of her eyes. He chuckled at her retort and snatched Barrett from her lap.

"Come on, boy. Let's find Ezra." He said and tossed Barrett on his shoulders. A cluster of lightning fired off overhead and Barrett covered his ears waiting for the thunder to explode.

"You're afraid of snakes Father?" Barrett asked Yori after the thunder was done.

"Yes, vial creatures." Yori patted Barrett's leg.

"We have something in common then huh, Father?" He yawned.

"Yes, son. I guess we do indeed." Yori said as they walked over to where Ezra and Asia stood.

******

Vada found Grayson laying in the grass with his arm across his eyes. She lowered to her hands and knees and slowly she tried to sneak up next to him. She squealed when he grabbed her and pulled her on top of him. She laughed out loud when he began to tickle her.

"Hello wife." He grinned. "That word is still foreign to my tongue, but I do like the sound of it." Grayson said touching her face softly. "You are so beautiful. How is it that I was chosen to be with you is a mystery I shall never understand."

"I believe it is I who is fortunate, my love. Do you not see how the other girls look at my husband with wanting eyes?

Least they be careful not to suffer my wrath." Vada warned with humor.

"My eyes do not wonder, Vada. Do you not know this?" Grayson pushed a string of her hair behind her ear.

"Aye husband I was just having a bit of fun." She stood and held out her hand to him. "Will you dance with me?" She asked as he stood. With the thunder as their beat Grayson put his arm around her waist and gently took her hand with the other. She lay her head against his neck and began to hum. Someone had seen them dancing and began playing a soft tune with his harmonica. Another with a string instrument. Ezra took Asia's hand and twirled her around and into his arms. Couples throughout the train joined them. Clara looked for Sara. She was standing close by watching the kids so in love as they danced in the meadow. Tears flowed down her face as she thought of Andrew and how he loved to dance, especially if it was storming. There was just something wonderful about a warm summer rain. She remembered a time Andrew rode in with wildflowers in his hand, swooped her from the porch and danced with her in the rain. She thought it was the most romantic gesture.

"That must be a very good memory judging from your smile and tears." Clara said, putting her arm around Sara's waist.

"He was such a good man, Clara." Sara turned to look at her friend. "What am I to do without him?"

"I don't know, but I will be here to help any way I can." Clara hugged her. "Look at our children Sara, look how in love they are. Our families are growing and soon we shall share grandchildren."

"How wonderful that will be." Sara smiled wiping away her tears. Suddenly, Vada went limp in Grayson's arms, and he caught her just before she fell to the ground.

"Vada!" Grayson shouted over the storm. He laid her gently on the ground. Sara and Clara heard his cry.

"She lost her ambulant. She's trying to shift." Sara told Clara as they ran toward them.

"What? It's too soon." Clara said worried as to what they would find once they reached them.

"Vada please open your eyes." Grayson begged, caressing her face with his fingertips. He looked up at Clara when she arrived. "Mother?" Grayson asked her for help. Clara and Sara knelt to assess Vada for change.

"Grayson, carry her to Sara's wagon." Clara instructed her son.

******

"It's time Ezra. You must get your people to the cave." Ezra heard a voice behind him but saw no one. He saw his brother carry Vada, limp in his arms across the meadow and looked at his father.

"We must go now." Ezra whistled for his horse and tossed Asia in the saddle. Lightning split the sky overhead as Ezra climbed on behind her. The rain let go with the thunderous crack that seemed to shake the ground. Grayson covered Vada and stuck Jenna under the blanket with her to watch her sister.

"Let me know if anything changes, ok Jenna?" Grayson asked with a wink.

"I will Grayson, I promise." Jenna said, placing her hand over her heart. Grayson mounted Vada's horse and pulled on his slicker. The rain was cold and icy as he rode to meet Ezra.

"We've got to find that cave quickly, I don't know what's happening with Vada, but this can't help." Grayson shouted over the rain.

"It's on the other side of those woods, but I don't know how thick they are." Ezra shouted back wiping the water from his eyes.

"Great more woods." Asia said annoyed.

"I'll get the pace picked up. You lead the way." Grayson said turning his horse back to the wagons. Ezra pulled his sword and held it in the air. The blue hue gave Yori a beacon to follow in the downpour they were riding in. When they reached the woods, it gave them a bit of a relief from the pounding, relentless rain. Urgency pushed them forward, and the knowledge that they were near the end of their journey kept them going. Ezra saw the cove from the top of the hill. He was overlooking the sea. They had made it. A path circled down the hill but there wasn't room for the wagons.

"You will have to walk from here. The cave is just down this hill, hurry." Ezra said waving them along. Grayson ran to Sara's wagon and helped her down. He handed Jenna down to her and then picked up Vada who was still unconscious. Grayson followed Sara and Jenna down the hill to the cave where Ezra placed his sword on the door. When the cave opened, they all hurried inside out of the chaotic weather. Exhausted, Grayson still carrying Vada slid down the wall of cave to the floor.

Worried about her he kissed her lips. "Please my love, awaken." The storm continued to beat the roof top of their shelter. Everyone was quiet listening to the rain and shivering from the cold.

"Place the sword in the rock." Ezra heard a whisper in his ear. He scanned the cave and found it in the center of the main room. Placing the tip of the sword into the rock, Ezra slid it down to the hilt. Gems and crystals lit up the cave. Asia was mesmerized by their beauty and reached out to touch one. The light from the gem struck her in the forehead and she collapsed onto the floor. Ezra ran for her and was hit by one of the many beams of colored light that bounced throughout the cave. He lost consciousness and dropped to the floor. One by one the adults succumbed to the gems light each collapsing into a deep sleep on the cave floor.

Vada woke first. She felt very strange. She tried to speak but it came out as a yip. She looked around her. There was a large black wolf asleep beside her and hundreds of dragons laying around the cave. Was this a dream? Had she hit her head and this was her delirium? She smelled the black wolf and he smelled of Grayson. What was going on? She nudged him until he woke. She spoke to him with her mind hoping he could hear and understand her. She licked his nose.

"Grayson, it's Vada. Do not make any sudden moves or you will wake the dragons." She looked into his eyes and she could tell he heard her. He tried to communicate but it came out a growl. "No, my love, use your mind to talk to me."

"Vada, why are we wolves? What happened? Where are we?" He tried to stand and stumbled.

"I don't know but I think we should get out of here before they all wake." Vada suggested and tested her footing. She seemed to pick up walking on four legs naturally, like she was born to it. "Grayson, we should go." She urged turning around to see he hadn't moved.

"This takes some concentration." He said shaking his shoulders. He finally, slowly moved around the dragons making it to the door. Grayson looked around the room at all of them. "I have never seen a dragon before."

"Well, you've never been a wolf before either but here we are." Vada said nipping at him. They walked down the path to the cove. There were existing buildings and homes down the coastline. A marvelous home that looked like it could have been for royalty stood at the end of the town road. A grand firepit was close by the castle like abode and strangely it was lit. There were no people about. They couldn't find their families anywhere. "Where is everyone?"

"I don't know if I like this, Vada. What if we never change back?" Grayson laid down by the fire pouting.

Vada lay beside him and licked his face. "At least we are together."

"I would like to know who's dream this nightmare belongs to, you or me." Grayson said laying his head down on his paws. Vada yawned and laid her head down. Sleep came to both and when they next woke, they were human.

"Grayson, we're back, and we're naked." She quickly looked to see if anyone was around to see.

Grayson looked at Vada from head to toe. "Now this dream is much to my liking."

"I am sure it is. But I am cold." She said covering her breasts and heading for the castle. "I hope there are clothes about."

"I am not especially in a hurry to cover just yet." Grayson smiled following her.

"I am sure you're not." Vada smiled over her shoulder. Inside the main house everything was clean of dust and in its place as if it was inhabited just moments ago. In one of the bedrooms Vada found a beautiful dark blue gown and held it in front of her for him to see.

"It is very pretty." Grayson said tossing the gown across the chair in the room. "But this, this is beautiful." He said looking over her body. "It has been days since our wedding night that I have been with you, wife, and there is no one about." He put his hand behind her neck and pulled her in close kissing her passionately. She felt the urge to be with him and pushed her hips against him. Grayson felt the wild nature of the wolf and the heat of the markings across his back and arms. He picked her up with one arm and laid her on the bed. A growl erupted within his chest as he touched her face and neck and she wrapped her legs around his waist positioning herself onto him. She threw her head back and raised her breast upward touching his chest. He groaned with the need to release. Grayson stopped for a moment and looked into her eyes.

"What is wrong, my love?" Vada asked with concern.

"I don't understand what is happening to us but, I just felt the need to tell you that I love you. You are forever my heart, Vada." Grayson kissed her tenderly.

"I love you, Grayson, the wolf and the man." She said placing both hands on each side of his face. He kissed her down her neck and nibbled on her skin. She raised her hips again to encourage him to continue. "I feel the warmth of you within, love." The sound of her soft whisper in his ear increased his pace. Grayson growled deeply as he grew close. She saw his fangs grow and the wolf in her responded. She mashed against his mouth with hers her fangs meeting his with fierce passion as they both peaked. They lay by one another kissing and gently touching. "What happened after I passed out." Vada asked, lacing her fingers into his.

"The rains poured down as Ezra rushed us to the cave. I carried you inside holding you close until the gems on the walls began to cast light across the rooms. Each beam seemed to target someone. I saw Asia fall first, then Ezra. When one found me, I slept. That's all I remember." Grayson answered touching her fangs.

She pulled his hand away. "Grayson, those dragons, they are our family, our friends! That cave has turned us." Grayson sat up realizing what she said was true.

"But why are we different? Why did we not become dragons with our family?" Grayson asked with confusion.

******

"Ezra, awaken." Ezra heard his name and felt someone touch his face. "Stay calm and listen to my voice." She said softly. "You are not in human form at the moment that is why you feel strange." She watched as he looked around at himself and the other dragons in the room.

"Asia?" Ezra tried to call out for her, but it came out as a screech. He looked at the entity and with irritation snorted out a puff of air.

"She is lying next to you." She said and nodded to where Asia still slept. "When you leave the cave, you will receive all the knowledge of past kings to be able to lead your people, Ezra. Close your eyes and concentrate on your human form. He did as she asked and was transformed back to himself. Ezra looked down at his clothes, they were royal attire. He had a crown upon his head and he took it off to look at it. "You are King. The kings and queens of the past have deemed you worthy of kingship. You are King Ezra, king of dragons." She curtsied.

"Why not my father? He is wiser than I." Ezra asked as she handed him back his sword.

"You don't give yourself enough credit young king. You are suited. You were chosen. Asia." She said to his wife and when she touched her face Asia's eyes opened quickly. She panicked at her appearance.

"Asia, be calm." The entity spoke, its voice was soothing as when it first addressed Ezra and helped her change to human form. Asia took Ezra's hand when he offered it to her.

"Ezra, I don't understand. Have I left my senses and live in another reality?" Asia asked and looked up at the crown he had on his head. "Was I a dragon? Are you now a king?"

He chuckled. "Yes and yes."

"You are their queen, Asia and Ezra their king. Together, you shall rule over the dragon people and bring forth a kingdom for all to live peacefully." The entity smiled then faded away into the crystal lit walls of the cave.

******

Vada and Grayson heard the screeching and crying of creatures unlike any they had ever heard before. Thunderous sounds of a storm that welded gusts of wind raged outside the castle door. Then they heard children laughing. Grayson opened the door to see that there was no storm. Cautiously, they walked outside. The laughter of the children was coming from the path to the cave with Barrett leading the way.

"Grayson!" He shouted, running toward his brother. He jumped up into his arms. "Look! They are all dragons!" Barrett pointed to the sky.

Jenna ran to Vada and hugged her. "There is Mother." She pointed to one of them. The other children gathered around the fire waiting for their parents to land. "Isn't it wonderful Vada?"

"Yes, Jenna it is." Vada smiled at her sister then looked at Grayson. They watched all the dragons land on the hilltop and as humans they walked down the road to where the children stood by the fire. Grayson stood by Vada and waited for their family. They saw Ezra and Asia hand in hand at the end of the line. Just in front of them were their parents.

Barrett ran to his mother with excitement. "Mother! You are a dragon! Will I get to be one too? Will I get to fly? What did it feel like? "

"Slow down Barrett." Yori laughed. "We cannot answer your questions yet. We barely know anything ourselves."

"Wow! Ezra has a crown! So does Asia!" Barrett looked at his father pointing at his brother.

"The entities of the cave made them our king and queen." Clara said looking at Grayson, his expression was hard to read. "Son, what is it?" She said walking over to him. She looked at Vada who lowered her eyes. "Grayson?"

"Mother, Vada and I were not made dragons. We are wolves." Grayson said and noticed no surprise on his mother's face. He tilted his head sideways when she looked away from him to Yori.

"Everyone!" Ezra shouted above the chatter. "It has been a very exciting, strange day to say the least. There are established homes made for us all along the coast and the hillside. Choose one for your families, then collect your things from your wagons. Tonight, we shall feast and celebrate our newly established sovereignty!" The people cheered, bowed and one by one they all left with their families to find a home. Ezra looked at Grayson confused at his demeanor. Vada shared the same confused expression. "Brother what causes your unhappiness? Is it my kingship?"

"No, Ezra. I have no quarrel with your entitlement." Grayson's eyes were black as was Vada's. "Vada and I were not made to be dragons. The cave's choice for us was wolves." Grayson sneered as his fangs grew. The fur collared black coat he wore made his frustration more ominous. Vada touched his arm and he calmed. "I am sorry, Ezra my disappointment is not directed at you intentionally." Grayson extended his arm and Ezra took it pulling his brother in he patted his back.

"We will figure it out together like we always do." Ezra whispered to him.

"So, king huh?" Grayson asked with a smirk.

"It seems so." Ezra shrugged, taking Asia's hand.

"Asia, you have made a beautiful queen." Vada curtsied and hugged her sister tightly.

"This is your home." Grayson said gesturing it with his hand. "We've already been inside. When we changed back, we were naked." Grayson laughed.

******

Tables were made from the wagons and set up in the road of the village. A wild boar was roasting on a pit and its aroma filled the cove teasing the hungry bellies of the people. Musicians brought out their stringed instruments and began to play while the ladies put the meals together. The children could be heard laughing and playing, enjoying their new home. Yori found his sons on top of the hill overlooking the water below. It was a beautiful place to be, this cove. An eagle screeched overhead and dove toward a fish that popped out of the water. Ezra had his hand on Grayson's shoulder, and they seemed to be engaged in a serious conversation.

"Vada and I feel it would be best." Grayson lowered his head. "Wolves and dragons do not mix, Ezra. This is all too new to everyone and I am sure that it would be better that they do not have to worry about wolves especially around the children."

"No, I won't have my family split up. There must be another way." Yori said looking from one to the other.

"Father, Vada and I were turned wolves. We know not what control we have over them as yet. It would be selfish and dangerous to stay until we understand more." Grayson turned and looked at his father with an expression of sadness.

"He is right Father." Ezra said. "At least for now. But tonight, we will feast." He smiled but was not happy. He didn't like the situation any more than Grayson did. "Come let's eat." Ezra led them down the path to the village center where the people were celebrating being home. As they walked along the road the people respectfully bowed to their new king. It was good to see them happy again.

******

Idris sat on his throne, listening to Samuel's report from Domminick. Suddenly, he stood and hurled his crown across the room in a fit of anger. "What do you mean he lost them? It was a wagon train, with hundreds of people, my people! You can't just loose a wagon train." Idris shouted as he paced the room.

"Sir Domminick stated that they traveled to what looked to be an ill-omened forest and as soon as Ezra disappeared into the fog, the woods just sort of imploded and was gone." Samuel said watching disbelief spread across the king's face. "He said it was as if they were being helped by things unworldly."

Idris looked at Samuel and snickered. It was not in humor. "Things unworldly. Sounds like the ramblings of a man who was desperate to keep his head. After all, losing a wagon train would certainly justify creating a marvelous magically tale then would it not?"

"I have never known Domminick to lie, my lord and he could have just as easily left with Ezra." Samuel answered shrugging his shoulders.

"He cannot leave because he is working off his father's debt knowing not that his father sits rotting in his cell as the rats gnaw on his bones. So, a longwinded story is not so far fetched to believe created." Idris waved his hand in front of himself dismissing his frustration. "I want them found, Samuel, send spies in all directions. No rest, until

Yori is dragged home." An unrest fell over Idris that day. Betrayal lingered, unforgiven.

******

Ezra and his family assembled in the dining hall of the royal manor before the festivities. Every face at the table held sadness that their family must separate at least for now.

"There has to be a way." Clara said looking at Ezra for an answer. "I do not want my children banished like some criminal."

"Mother, all of this is too new. We know absolutely nothing about how Grayson and Vada are as wolves. I do not want this no more than you or them but for now I must agree with Grayson that it is what is best for this kingdom for the moment." Ezra answered calmly but frustrated. Grayson took Vada's hand and smiled at her. "At least we will be warm this winter."

"Nothing like a fur coat on a cold day huh my love." Vada said taking his hand when he offered it to her.

"What about you?" Grayson spoke to everyone. "How was it waking up as a dragon?"

"I would venture to say just as surprising as it was for you waking as a wolf." Asia said looking over at Grayson and smiled. "It took a little bit of time to get the wings working right."

"I am not sure it is for me." Yori said shaking his head. "I am not crazy about heights."

Ezra's mind was already thinking and strategizing. "I would like to visit with the elders of the neighboring villages and begin a trust between us. I think we could benefit from their alliances. In past lives I believe it was custom of the ancient dragon Kings and Queens to be protection for all the villages within the realm." Ezra said sitting back in his chair tapping the table with his finger.

"I think it is awesome!" Barrett shouted. "I can't wait to fly. How long will it be before I get to be a dragon? Will I breathe fire? Ezra? Am I a prince?" Everyone laughed releasing worry, tension, and anxiety that had been building for some time.

Ezra and Asia followed their family out to join their community for the celebration of arriving at the cove. He took his wife's hand and stood at the end of the table.

"Welcome home everyone!" Ezra shouted holding up a goblet. Cheers echoed up and down the streets of their new market. "It seems the children have been enjoying the cove so far." Children's voices could be heard screaming in agreement. "Not only have we found a new kingdom to call home, but we have awakened as more than just mere mortals. Not in our wildest dreams did we figure to rise from the cave as dragons. I believe that our destiny is to protect those around us and this cove from any force that threatens to destroy this beautiful place and the people in it." Ezra waited for the cheers to quieten before speaking again. "It is an honor to be chosen as your king and to rule a peaceful nation with Queen Asia at my side! Now, enjoy this wonderful feast that has blessed our tables and sleep soundly in your beds tonight."

"Long live King Ezra!" Grayson stood raising his goblet. "Long live Queen Asia!" The people joined in repeating Grayson. Ezra looked at Grayson holding his cup up to his. There was pride in Grayson's smile as he looked at his brother the king. "Long live you brother."

"And also, you brother." Ezra smiled back at him.

******

Asia stood on the hillside looking over the cliff at the beautiful cove. The water gently slapped the rocks below as it pushed ashore with a gently soothing tone. The flap of dragon's wings echoed over her as she soaked up the warm spring sun. A little bit of a breeze swayed her hair back and forth on her back, and a strand whipped around into her face. After brushing it away she pulled back the blanket to look upon her daughter's face. Ezra slipped up behind her and wrapped his arms around her waist looking over her shoulder at their babe.

"I thought I might find you up here." He said kissing the side of her head.

"It is so peaceful." She said rubbing his hand.

"Yes, it is my love." He took his daughter from Asia smiling down at her.

"She is so beautiful. I can't believe I am a father." Ezra held her in the crook of his arm and pointed at the world around them. "Welcome my daughter to Dragon's Cove."

THE BEGINNING

www.ingramcontent.com/pod-product-compliance
Lightning Source LLC
LaVergne TN
LVHW021802060526
838201LV00058B/3207